SWEET VALLEY UNIVERSITY®

Spy Girl

Written by
Laurie John

Created by
FRANCINE PASCAL

BANTAM BOOKS
NEW YORK • TORONTO • LONDON • SYDNEY • AUCKLAND

RL 8, age 14 and up

SPY GIRL

A Bantam Book / November 1997

Sweet Valley High® and Sweet Valley University®
are registered trademarks of Francine Pascal.
Conceived by Francine Pascal.
Produced by Daniel Weiss Associates, Inc.
33 West 17th Street
New York, NY 10011.

ISBN: 0-553-57058-7

Published simultaneously in the United States and Canada

Bantam Books are published by Bantam Books, a division of Bantam Doubleday Dell Publishing Group, Inc. Its trademark, consisting of the words "Bantam Books" and the portrayal of a rooster, is Registered in U.S. Patent and Trademark Office and in other countries. Marca Registrada. Bantam Books, 1540 Broadway, New York, New York 10036.

PRINTED IN THE UNITED STATES OF AMERICA

OPM 0 9 8 7 6 5 4 3 2 1

To Kacey Michelle Cotton

Chapter One

"That's it!" Tom Watts cried, leaping from his seat in front of the microfiche machine in the Sweet Valley University library. He did a little victory dance as a short newspaper article concerning the Verona Springs Country Club printed out. "Now I've got you, Elizabeth Wakefield!" he crowed to himself triumphantly. "It took all night, but I've finally found it!"

And just in time, he realized with a start as he glanced up at the library clock. He was supposed to be meeting his roommate, Danny Wyatt, at the University Center for breakfast in ten minutes.

"Hey!" a gruff voice hissed from the next table. "Save the rain dance for the next drought. Some of us are trying to study!"

Tom froze, blushing beet red as he realized that the eyes of at least half a dozen of his fellow SVU students were on him. *Whoops!* The high-tech research room in the library basement wasn't exactly a partying kind of place—more like a hangout for the ultra-serious set, especially on a Monday morning.

Tom grinned sheepishly, tucking in the back of his light-blue polo shirt before slipping—nonchalantly, he hoped—back into his metal chair. "Sorry about that," he whispered. But Tom couldn't help being proud; he'd just made *the* discovery that had been eluding him since yesterday afternoon.

He uncapped his ballpoint pen and quickly jotted down some notes on his experiences during the last twenty-four hours. He'd been on a date at the Verona Springs Country Club with Dana Upshaw when he'd run into his ex-girlfriend, Elizabeth Wakefield. Elizabeth was at the club with Scott Sinclair, her new reporting partner at the *Sweet Valley Gazette*—and, it seemed, her new boyfriend as well.

Tom gritted his teeth, momentarily reliving the anger and frustration he'd felt at the possessive way Scott had held Elizabeth's hand. Even though his own feelings about Dana were mixed, he'd thrown his arm around her in unspoken retaliation. He felt an uncomfortable knot growing in his stomach at the memory. Was he being fair to Dana?

Stick to the relevant facts, Watts, his reporter's instinct silently growled at him. *A real journalist doesn't let his personal feelings interfere with his work.*

Tom sighed and focused on the notebook before him. *So there we were—Dana and I, Elizabeth and Scott—standing in the Verona Springs Country Club garden maze,* he recalled. Suddenly, an elderly Latino gardener had appeared out of nowhere and uttered what had sounded like a cryptic warning.

"Go home," he'd said after discovering that they were all SVU students. "Go back to school. . . . Go away from this place."

Tom felt himself getting excited all over again. This was his favorite part of being a reporter—the first scent of a story. Elizabeth had seemed to understand right away what the gardener had meant and had begun to pepper the old man with questions—out of earshot, naturally. When Tom had tried to get in on the action, the gardener had disappeared.

"But now *I* know what the old guy was referring to too," he murmured with satisfaction. "Take *that,* Miss High-and-Mighty!"

Tom ran a strong hand through his thick, dark brown hair as he studied the photocopy of the article he'd found. STUDENT HELD FOR QUESTIONING, read the small headline. The story had been practically buried on page 32 of a week-old issue of the *Southern California Sun.*

"No wonder it took me all night to find it," Tom mused. "The country club must have used its influence to keep this story as quiet as possible."

He slowly scanned the article, reviewing the facts one more time. Brandon Phillips, an SVU junior, was being held for questioning regarding the death by drowning of Dwayne Mendoza, a classmate and fellow Verona Springs caddy. Mendoza's body had been found in the Verona Springs Reservoir, and some unnamed objects belonging to Mendoza were found in Phillips's possession. No other details were given. No indication of whether the cops suspected Phillips of murder—or even if it was a murder to begin with.

Tom juggled the facts in the article and Elizabeth's behavior at the country club in his mind. When he put it all together, it looked like an open-and-shut case. Hard as it was to believe that one SVU student had robbed and killed another, it seemed even more difficult to explain how such a brutal crime could have been covered up as well as this one had. To the best of Tom's knowledge, there wasn't a single person at SVU—except for Elizabeth and Scott, of course—who was aware that these events had taken place.

But maybe it isn't as open-and-shut as it looks, his reporter's instinct argued. *Why else would that gardener be so nervous?*

And why else would Elizabeth be so interested?

Tom felt a small trickle of fear start down his spine. Being an investigative journalist wasn't always the safest extracurricular activity. *Will following this story put Elizabeth in danger?* he wondered uneasily.

For a brief moment, his heart flipped over in his chest as he imagined her lovely features twisted in terror. Quickly he shook his pity away. There once was a time when he would rather have died than imagine anything or anyone hurting Elizabeth. Before their nasty breakup—when they'd been partners at WSVU, the campus television station—Tom had always been there for her. Not that Elizabeth couldn't take care of herself—Tom knew all too well how capable she was of that now. But he'd have taken on any threat to keep Elizabeth safe and protected.

"Not anymore," Tom murmured, shoving his hands into the pockets of his chinos and slumping down into his chair. "Now it's war. It's me against Elizabeth—"

And Scott Sinclair, a cruel, taunting voice in his mind finished. Tom clenched his fists, barely suppressing the urge to ball up the *Sun* article that lay on the desk before him.

"Scott Sinclair," he hissed. "Not only can Elizabeth take care of herself, but she's a fast worker too."

Tom grabbed his notebook and papers and started to shove them into his knapsack. How did he allow himself to get so hung up on Elizabeth Wakefield in the first place anyway? It was obvious she had a fickle heart. Barely two weeks had passed since he'd seen her tramping around the quad with Todd Wilkins.

Tom ducked his head, his face burning with the memory of finding Elizabeth and her ex locked in a passionate embrace right outside the WSVU building. Tom had thought she was running to see *him*, but . . .

But . . .

But whose fault is that, Tom? he thought grimly. You *were the one who rejected her.* You *were the one who refused to believe her when she told you about your father's unwanted advances.*

Tom shook his head sadly. "I couldn't help it, Liz," he whispered. "And if anybody can understand why, it should be you."

He'd always had a searing emptiness in his heart after losing the man he'd thought of as Dad—and the rest of his family—in a tragic car crash during his freshman year. When Elizabeth had reunited him with his biological father, George Conroy, and he'd realized he had a half brother and sister, it was as if he'd been given a new lease on life. He had a family again! Believing Elizabeth's story about his biological father's inappropriate behavior toward her would have meant losing that family too.

Now it had turned out that Elizabeth had been telling the truth. George Conroy really *had* been sexually obsessed with her.

Tom blinked back the shameful memory of his disbelief of Elizabeth's story—and how horribly he'd treated her afterwards. He'd tried to make it up to her by writing her a letter begging her to forgive him. He'd left the letter in her basket on her WSVU desk.

The next day, when he saw her long, blond hair streaming behind her as she ran toward the station, he'd assumed she was on her way to accept his apology and maybe even take him back.

"What a fool I was," he growled, remembering what he'd seen instead. "Of all the times and places she could have chosen to fall in Wilkins's arms, she chose then and there. She did it to rub it in my face and let me know my feelings meant nothing to her. And the only reason she set foot inside WSVU at all was to pack up her stuff and leave."

I'm going after this story, Elizabeth, he thought bitterly. *If you can trample my heart without a second thought, then I can trample you professionally!*

"When you kissed me, Scott, that was totally out of line." Elizabeth Wakefield stared down into her fresh cup of coffee, her second this morning, and took a deep breath before continuing. "All the other stuff—the touching, the friendly little hugs—even though I didn't always feel one hundred percent comfortable, I could still deal with it. But that kiss yesterday . . . that just wasn't right. I don't feel that way about you, Scott. I don't."

Elizabeth drummed her fingers anxiously on the table in the crowded University Center and waited for Scott Sinclair's apology. He owed her one, no matter what excuse he had brewing in his sharp, savvy mind. Ever since Scott had first convinced her to leave WSVU and return to print journalism at the *Sweet Valley Gazette*, he had always been friendly—a little *too* friendly, perhaps. And now that they were embroiled in an investigation that required them to pose as a couple, Scott had taken the act too far.

When they'd returned to campus after snooping around the Verona Springs Country Club yesterday afternoon, Scott had forcefully kissed Elizabeth—even after she'd told him to stop it. In his defense, Scott had insisted that they needed to pose as a couple. But that trail of logic didn't hold up when the manicured lawns of Verona Springs were nowhere in sight.

She'd rushed home, even though she'd hoped to get some serious work done on the story—*her* story—exposing the circumstances surrounding the mysterious death of Dwayne Mendoza, a Verona Springs caddy and SVU student. But she couldn't bear being around Scott a minute longer. After pacing the floors until the carpet was virtually threadbare, she'd called Scott and arranged an emergency breakfast meeting in the University Center coffee shop to clear the air.

Scott took a long drink from his cup and gulped, pausing thoughtfully before turning his crystalline blue eyes to meet hers. "I'm so sorry,

Elizabeth. You're right. It was wrong of me to . . . to take advantage of you that way. I didn't know—"

"That's right, you didn't know," Elizabeth interrupted calmly but forcefully. She wanted to maintain some level of disappointment in her voice so that he'd be certain of just how upset she was, even though the sincerity in his voice was breaking down her defenses. "But now you do. And that means we have to draw the line when it comes to physical contact between us."

"Whoa, but what about the investigation?" Scott argued, holding his hands in front of him as if deflecting a blow. "We can't just *not* pretend to be dating, Liz. If we do that, our cover will be blown. There'll be no way we'll be allowed into the Couples Only section of the club—and that's our only way in, remember?"

Elizabeth rubbed her sleep-deprived eyes in amazement. Didn't Scott *ever* give up? *I guess that's what makes him a good reporter,* she thought, only half-bemused. *He's as persistent as a rash sometimes.* "Like I told you once before," she began pointedly, "I don't think the jet set appreciates public displays of affection all that much. We'll do what we have to do, Scott, but *within reason*. And when we're on campus—"

"Hands off," Scott finished.

"Exactly." Elizabeth nodded and smiled thankfully. "You're learning."

"Guess so." Scott turned his handsome face

toward the floor-to-ceiling windows lining the University Center and squinted into the bright morning sunshine streaming through. After a long, careful silence, he turned back to her and gave her a respectful look. "So I suppose we should move on to the story now . . . if you think you're ready."

"Yes," Elizabeth replied emphatically. "We've got to hustle, or else we'll get scooped." She winced slightly at the memory of running into Tom Watts and Dana Upshaw at the country club the day before. The idea that he could be working towards nabbing her story as they spoke drove a dagger through her heart.

"About that gardener . . . ," Scott began, snapping his fingers as if trying to recall the name.

"Juan Mendoza," Elizabeth supplied, switching effortlessly into dedicated journalist mode. "Dwayne's uncle. We've *got* to get him to talk to us, Scott." She took a quick glance around the noisy University Center as if thinking about the elderly man might make him miraculously appear. But the strong morning light revealed only tables full of chattering students who sipped coffee and nibbled pastries. Still, Mr. Mendoza's strange words of warning echoed in her mind.

"It is not safe here. Some people think . . . they can get away with murder."

Murder! She shivered a little before turning her attention back to Scott, who was staring at her intently, as if hanging on her next thought or word. "We need to win his confidence," she went on, "so he'll tell us more about what happened the night his nephew was found dead."

"Exactly!" Scott made a move to reach across the table for her hand, but stopped himself, smiling apologetically. "That's totally ingenious."

Elizabeth leaned back in her wooden chair and crossed her arms. "That wasn't exactly a brainstorm, Scott," she teased.

He laughed and tucked a strand of his shoulder-length blond hair behind one ear. "I guess you're right. It's just . . . I'm so glad this assignment at Verona Springs is turning out to be a *real* story and not just the puff piece our noble editor-in-chief wanted."

Elizabeth grinned and smoothed down the crease in her long navy blue skirt. "I'm sure Ed knows what he's doing. He just wanted to make my switch back into print a little easier." She took a sip of her coffee. "He assigned me a puff piece to get me started, that's all."

Scott shook his head. "You? Need to get *started*? No way. Journalism is in your blood. Just because you wasted—I mean, *spent* some of your time chasing sound bites for WSVU doesn't mean you've lost your writing talent."

Elizabeth blushed and shrugged at the same time. She couldn't help but feel flattered by Scott's praise. Since they'd met not a day had gone by without him telling her how much he admired her reporting abilities. Becoming a professional journalist had always been her dream, and it was nice to hear her talents commended. Especially since the person most intimate with her work did nothing but treat her with disrespect.

Tom Watts, Elizabeth thought bleakly, her face clouding over. *He used to be my biggest supporter. Now he's my biggest competitor.*

"Elizabeth, are you all right?" Scott asked kindly. "I hope you don't feel that there's too much pressure on you on your return to print."

Elizabeth focused on Scott's handsome, concerned features. "No, I'm fine," she said, shaking the image of Tom's sneering face from her mind. "I'm glad for the challenge. I was never very good with articles that were all show and no substance anyway. If all we were writing about was a silly little country club tennis tournament, it would have been a lot harder for me."

Scott smiled. "Me too."

"What?" She laughed, tossing back her long blond ponytail. "*I* was assigned this story. *You* only volunteered to come along for the ride."

Scott gave a sheepish grin and toyed with the collar of his green-and-white striped button-down shirt. "Well, you needed a boyfriend to gain entry to the Couples Only section, where the tournament was taking place."

Boyfriend? Elizabeth raised one eyebrow.

"Scott, I can think of a half-dozen stories that would have utilized your talents *much* better—and a half-dozen other male reporters at the *Gazette* who could have *easily* taken your place."

Elizabeth's retort seemed to hit Scott like a .44 caliber bullet. His Adam's apple bobbed guiltily as he cleared his throat and hurriedly reached for his leather satchel. "Now let me see . . . where did I put those notes?"

Suppressing a grin of victory, Elizabeth reached for her coffee cup and took a sip, studying Scott over the rim as he looked through his case. No denying it—he *was* extremely handsome, with a classic Greek profile, wavy, sun-streaked blond hair, and bright blue eyes. Unfortunately, he had an unwelcome habit of stepping into her personal space. *At this point in my life, I'm not ready for* anything *personal*, she mused, *except . . .*

Elizabeth shook the thought away. *Get out of my head, Tom. You're off limits to me now,* she scolded silently. *You made that perfectly clear yesterday when you jumped on my story like it was a trampoline—not to mention the fact that you were all over that ditz Dana Upshaw. The battle lines have been drawn. This is war!*

"I'm going to throttle that Sinclair creep in a minute," Tom growled. "What does Elizabeth see in him?" He glared past Danny Wyatt's close-cropped black hair at the happy little couple, who were nestled cozily on the other side of the crowded University Center coffee shop and spoiling his appetite. Breakfast with his roommate usually meant a chance for Tom to relax. But today the hot coffee was fast turning sour in the pit of his stomach.

"Don't let him get to you, Tom," Danny advised, scratching one of his toned biceps through the sleeve of his white T-shirt. "It's not worth it."

"I know, man. But I can't help it." Tom winced as Scott's tone of voice got even louder and more aggressive.

"TV journalism is such a waste of time, you know?" his obnoxious voice bellowed. "*Real* reporters like you and me, Liz—we have the heart and the talent to go in-depth and really get to know the people behind the stories. We're tuned in to what makes them tick, how they feel. Sound bites just can't cut it. No matter how brilliant and noble the TV reporter *thinks* he is, he's bound to fail miserably."

Tom's hand shook with barely controlled anger as he lifted his mug to his lips.

Danny's jet-black eyes flashed him a warning look. "Just ignore him, Watts, or you'll end up turning that new blue shirt into an old coffee-stained rag."

Tom glowered. "I'd rather pour it down the front of *his* shirt. Or, better yet, use this mug to plug up his big mouth."

Danny snorted. "Well, you can prove that clown wrong by scooping this country club story. I'd hate to see you end up behind bars for aggravated assault. Now pass me the milk, please."

Tom pushed the tiny pitcher toward his friend before crossing his arms. "You just gave me a great idea, Danny," he began. "Why don't we wait until tonight, when there aren't any witnesses around? Then we can get a bunch of guys together and jump him from behind."

"Tom!" Danny spluttered, practically spitting his coffee out of his mouth.

Tom's face broke into a devilish grin as he tossed Danny a napkin. "Kidding, Danny-O," he said with a laugh. But his joke turned sour in his mind when he remembered how Danny's older brother, Thad, had been left wheelchair-bound after a crippling knife fight. Danny hated violence of any kind—even in jokes.

"Not funny, Watts," Danny exhorted.

"I know, man," Tom replied, shamefaced. "Sorry."

Danny nodded. "That's OK. But you're beginning to make me nervous here, Tommo. Remember that night at the Delta Chi party when you were chug-a-lugging like a maniac? I wouldn't have put a stunt like that past you then."

Tom felt instantly ashamed at the memory. After the breakup with Elizabeth, he'd made an ill-fated attempt to drown his sorrows by trying on his old, party-hearty Wildman Watts persona from his freshman year. It hadn't worked. He'd only ended up with a raging hangover and a guilty conscience that would take years to heal.

"That was a mistake," Tom said quietly. "I've learned my lesson. Wildman Watts is dead and buried. I *won't* be reviving that caveman again. *Ever.*"

Danny stared at him for a moment and then nodded. "Good. I like Pulitzer Prize Winner Watts much better." He stood and scooped up his textbooks. "I've got to get a move on. I promised Izzy I'd meet her before our ten o'clock class."

"That's cool," Tom replied, feeling a twinge of jealousy at how his roommate's relationship with gorgeous Isabella Ricci had stood the test of time, while his own seemingly perfect romance with Elizabeth had flopped. "Later."

As Danny strolled off, Tom pushed his feelings aside and turned back to his coffee. He was just about to take another gulp when Sinclair's voice again rose above the other students' chatter.

"TV journalism is for hacks," he practically shouted. "Hollywood wanna-bes without the depth of perception or understanding of craft necessary to make any meaningful contribution to the information marketplace. As you said, Elizabeth, it's all show and no substance."

Tom froze. Sinclair blasting TV journalism was one thing. But Elizabeth? He shot a furious look over to where the two of them were sitting. Their heads were so close that they could have been kissing.

I don't have to sit here and take this, Tom thought furiously, tapping a spoon against his coffee cup hard enough to crack it.

"That's not what I meant at all, Scott," Elizabeth insisted, squirming in her seat uncomfortably. *Why is Scott acting like such a jerk?* she wondered. *We've been through the whole superiority-of-print-over-TV thing a million times. Who's he trying to impress? It certainly can't be me.*

Elizabeth lifted her hand to make another point, causing a fork to clatter to the floor. When she bent to pick it up, she noticed Tom sitting across the room, a venomous, don't-push-me look contorting his features. When their eyes met, Tom jumped to his feet.

Her breath catching in her throat, Elizabeth jerked up in her seat and attempted to act as if she hadn't seen anything. But she knew it was futile. Scott had obviously spotted Tom long before she had; *that's* why he had launched into his tired old tirade.

She bit back a sigh of annoyance and twisted her napkin between her hands. *How dare Scott do this to me?* she asked herself. *I don't think I can handle another public confrontation with Tom.* Her heart beat rapidly as she searched for a way out.

Maybe if I put up a verbal fight, Tom will leave me alone for once.

"You know, Liz, it's all about—"

"Hold it, Scott," Elizabeth interrupted hotly, praying her voice reached Tom's ears. "When I was talking about substance versus show, I was referring to choice of story, *not* print over TV."

Scott waved her remark away. "Of course, Elizabeth. But that was a sterling example of what we've been talking about. Print being the realm of the real journalist, TV mere show."

Elizabeth hazarded a glance in Tom's direction. To her relief, he was preparing to leave, gathering up his tray and flinging his knapsack over his broad shoulders. But those shoulders slumped pathetically as he strode toward the exit of the University Center. Tom turned to give Elizabeth one last withering look before he left. But it wasn't a look of hate—it was one of hurt.

She almost cried out as Tom's eyes bore through her, touching her very soul. Even though Tom had dumped her, denied her, and went out of his way to make her miserable, she couldn't help it: When he was in pain, she was too.

Hastily, without even thinking, Elizabeth got to her feet. "If you'll excuse me," she hissed at Scott, grabbing her blue gabardine jacket from the back of her chair. Ignoring Scott's stunned expression, she pulled on her jacket and took off in pursuit of her ex-boyfriend.

"Tom!" she cried, weaving through the crowded tables and pushing open the large glass University Center doors, squinting as the sunlight of the bright, clear California morning met her eyes.

Tom kept walking, his dark head of wavy brown hair bowed, his hands shoved deep into the pockets of his chinos. From behind he looked as if he were fighting against a storm front, not striding into a warm, sunny day.

"Tom, wait!"

Tom whipped around to stare at her, his brown eyes blazing. "What do you want, Elizabeth? Didn't get enough cracks in over coffee? Or is it only fun when the object of your ridicule is sitting a few tables away?"

Elizabeth stopped in her tracks. Tom's chiseled face was drawn down into a churlish scowl. The hurt she'd seen there was gone, replaced by venomous rage. "I . . . ," she trailed off, feeling the fury coming off of him in waves. "I didn't know you were . . ."

"Don't backpedal on me," Tom sneered. "And don't apologize either. I don't accept apologies from blowhard amateurs. I'm twice the journalist you or Sinclair will ever be."

Elizabeth took an angry step toward him, her hands flying to her hips. *What a jerk!* she thought. *Scott must have hit Tom pretty hard for him to get defensive like this. Well, he doesn't have to take it out on me. But if that's how he wants it—fine!*

"Drop the tough-guy act, Tom," she demanded. "We're miles ahead of you on this story. And there's no way you're going to guilt me into *helping* you. You're *toast.*"

Tom fumbled with his knapsack, pulled a copy of an article from the *Southern California Sun* out, and thrust it in her face. "Not anymore, Elizabeth. I don't *need* your help. I know what you two know—probably more. You and Sinclair can go ahead and spend all the time you want knocking TV journalism. Meanwhile, I'll be out landing this story."

"You mean *my* story, Tom," Elizabeth snapped back. "And I promise you that *I'm* going to crack it first. I'll knock you down from your pedestal if it's the last thing I do!"

She turned on her heels and stormed back toward the swinging glass doors. She had a job to do, and that didn't include standing outside the University Center being insulted by Tom Watts. What it *did* include was getting back in touch with Juan Mendoza—and finding out who the subject of the article headed STUDENT HELD FOR QUESTIONING was.

Thought you were one step ahead of me, Tom? Elizabeth asked silently, a sly smile spreading across her face. *Unfortunately for you, you forgot one of the cardinal rules of journalism: Never show off your research to the competition!*

* * *

Oh, no! Lila Fowler thought anxiously as she peered over her expensive designer sunglasses. Pepper Danforth and Bunny Sterling, the two most powerful members of the Verona Springs Country Club, were heading straight toward her. They looked like they meant business. But what business could they possibly have?

Lila carefully placed her glass of iced tea on the small ceramic table next to her poolside deck chair and quickly fluffed up her chestnut brown hair. "Maybe they've made *Bruce* their business," she gasped in horror. "Of course! They're going to finally boot Bruce and me out of the club over the appalling way he treated Bunny!"

Lila moaned and dropped her head into her hands. Bruce had told her all about his one awful blind date with Bunny and his terrible behavior toward her when she wouldn't leave him alone for weeks afterward. He had deliberately ditched her at the Sigma house, drunk. He'd claimed to have joined the Olympic triathlon team, which "required" him to move to the Andes in order to train in a high-altitude environment. He'd finally told Bunny off so insensitively—and publicly—that she'd thrown a rock through a Sigma house window in humiliation. And even though Bunny had moved on and gotten engaged to Paul Krandall, a congressman's son who was probably as dim as he was privileged, Lila still feared the inevitable payback.

"Of all the girls to treat so badly, he *had* to choose someone essential to our social future," she whispered angrily. "We'll be pariahs if we don't become Verona Springs VIPs! I'll have to join a convent!"

Lila gulped, her brown eyes darting anxiously in search of an escape route. If she leapt from her deck chair right now, maybe she could make it to the trees at the edge of the golf course before they saw her.

No way! Her high heeled sandals would sink into the soft grass and she'd be trapped for sure. What about the pool in front of her? She could dive into the deep end and hold her breath until she turned blue. But that would mean getting her brand new Alain of Montauk swimsuit all wet! And anyway, the water was crystal clear—Pepper and Bunny would be sure to see her there.

A fit of nervous giggles started forming in the pit of Lila's stomach. Her last option was to flee into the clubhouse and hope to lose herself in one of the large, opulently decorated rooms. But even then she'd be seen. The windows were huge and kept spotlessly clean at all times. *No,* Lila realized, *I'm going to have to face the music . . . no matter how bad it sounds.*

"Luh-*iii*-luh-ah," Pepper drawled, somehow able to draw four full syllables out of the name. "There you are, *darling*. We've been looking all over for you." She bent down and kissed the air next to Lila's ear.

An excitable hiccup escaped from Lila's lips.

"What was that, dear?" Pepper asked, raking long, flawlessly manicured fingernails through her white-blond hair.

Lila felt her face turning crimson. "Nothing," she squeaked, desperately trying to swallow down the next hiccup and the fretful titters that were bursting to follow it. *Hmmm . . . maybe I should go blond too,* she thought, forcing herself to concentrate on more positive matters. *I wonder who Pepper's colorist is?*

"Lovey, you'd better get out of the sun," Bunny declared with a toothy smile. "You're turning boiled lobster red. Daddy would *never* cast a girl in a movie who's boiled lobster red."

Pepper raised one rail-thin arm to shield her eyes. "Really, Lila, *why* do it the old-fashioned way? They have *excellent* sun beds next to the sauna. I mean, *look* at *me*." She pushed up the sleeve of her electric green polo top to show a patch of orangy skin.

"*Perfect* tone," Bunny simpered. "Daddy would *looove* your skin, Pep." She nodded as she adjusted the hem of her tight, nausea-inspiring minidress. It was covered with a vile fluorescent paisley pattern that somehow brought to mind a sea of radioactive parasites.

Lila smiled sweetly, still fighting her anxiety-driven urge to laugh. Bunny's oversized head was bobbing so feverishly, Lila was sure that it was about to topple off her skinny frame. *How can such an undernourished body support a huge weight like that?* she wondered. *Wait, I remember—her head's not heavy at all. There's nothing but air inside it!*

"Anyway," Pepper said, dropping down onto the chair next to Lila's, "Bunny and I have some business to discuss with you."

I knew it, Lila thought. *We're out. I'm going to kill you, Bruce Patman!* Even though Bunny was an absolute fright, Lila had nothing but the highest respect for Pepper. As junior president of the VIP Circle, Pepper had the power to yea or nay anyone's entrance into the exclusive group. Ever since she had discovered that fact, Lila had gone on a mission to flatter Pepper by emulating her in every way possible: buying the same designer clothing she bought, wearing the same nail color she wore, even using the same hair spray she used. *Bleaching my hair to match Pepper's may be* too *much of a good thing,* she suddenly realized, momentarily distracted. *Perhaps her colorist could just give me some nice streaks.*

"Now, I *know* this is short notice," Pepper chattered gaily, breaking through her thoughts, "seeing as how the event starts this afternoon and all, but . . ." She smiled sweetly, her white, capped teeth gleaming in the sunshine. "We'd like *you* to organize the pairings for the VIP mixed doubles tournament."

Bunny squealed. "Oooh. Isn't that just the *best* honor? Daddy would think that's the best honor. Aren't you just *so* excited?"

Lila felt her mouth drop open and a huge weight lift from her slender shoulders. "Yes," she gushed, breaking out into a huge, relieved grin. "I'm thrilled. Wait till I tell Bruce!"

"Bruce will be *so* pleased," Pepper breathed.

"Mmm-hmm." Bunny nodded supportively. "Bruce will be just so very, very pleased. *Ciao*!" She turned on one hot-pink-sandalled heel and sauntered away.

Pepper got up and followed her friend. "*Ciao,* darling."

"Ciao!" Lila chirped, basking in the glow of relief. She and Bruce weren't going to be kicked out of anything. Far from it. They were practically being offered two guaranteed seats in the VIP Circle!

Leaning back in her deck chair, she picked up her glass of iced tea and sipped it, taking care not to muss her Fuschia Frost lipstick—Pepper's favorite color. *Sweet, sweet victory,* she thought. *It's mine—all mine!*

"Here it is!" Elizabeth murmured excitedly as page 32 of the *Southern California Sun* came into view on the microfiche reader. The tiny headline STUDENT HELD FOR QUESTIONING shone out from the screen like a beam of hope.

"'Brandon Phillips, twenty, a junior at Sweet Valley University, is being held for questioning in the drowning death of Dwayne Mendoza, nineteen, a fellow junior at SVU,'" Scott read aloud. "'Mendoza's body was found early this week in the reservoir of the Verona Springs Country Club, where both men worked as caddies. While several items belonging to Mendoza were found in Phillips's possession, no charges have yet been filed in the case, nor will police comment on the nature of Mendoza's death.'" Scott shook his head. "Boy, *that's* helpful. That doesn't give us anything."

"Yes it does!" Elizabeth hissed under her breath, amazed at Scott's lack of perception. "Brandon Phillips . . . don't you see? The police actually approached someone for questioning. Perhaps Phillips knows something . . ."

"Or maybe he killed Mendoza." Scott nodded. "You're right. We've got to move on this. You should call the cops and—"

"I can't," Elizabeth admitted, her heart sinking. "My sister's boyfriend is a police detective. If he finds out that I'm investigating this story, he's sure to tell my sister. And then *she'll* be all over this story like white on rice. We've already got too many people hovering around the club as it is."

"You're right." Scott rubbed his hand over his chin in thought. "Tell you what, Liz. I'll handle it. I'm pretty good at wringing information out of people—especially those who don't want to give any up."

"OK," Elizabeth conceded, even though deep down, she wasn't so sure. *Please don't mess this up, Scott,* she prayed silently. *If you get tripped up by the police, our story will be history.*

"Should I call them now?" Scott asked, breaking through her thoughts.

"No," Elizabeth replied decisively. "We've got to go to the club and find Juan Mendoza first. Who knows? After we talk to him, we may not need this Phillips guy at all."

"Pick up, Jess," Nick Fox murmured as Jessica Wakefield's dorm room phone continued to ring. He leaned back in his squeaky leather desk chair at the Sweet Valley police station and studied the clock on the wall. Nearly eleven-thirty. He'd been out until three A.M. on a stakeout and then back at work by seven. Was Jessica still sleeping? He knew she liked her beauty rest, but this would be a record even by her standards.

Nick felt a warm glow travel through his broad chest as he imagined Jessica sleeping soundly beneath her purple satin comforter, one slender arm flung across her angelic features. How such a sweet looking creature could cause so much trouble, he couldn't begin to imagine. "But I wouldn't change one golden hair on her head for all the predictability in the world," he whispered.

"Hey, Fox." Bill Fagen, one of Nick's fellow detectives, looked up from his desk. "I hear you talking to yourself over there. Are you going batty? Because if you are, I'll take that blond bombshell off your hands."

Nick chuckled and stroked the stubble on his chiseled jaw. "The day I gave up Jessica would be the day I lost my mind."

"Hello?" a sleepy voice breathed on the other end of the line.

Nick felt a wide smile creep across his face. "Hi, sunshine, it's almost eleven-thirty. Did you have a hard night?"

Jessica groaned. "Hardly. While you were having fun catching criminals, I was home alone. Bored out of my mind."

Nick grinned. "It can't be that bad. I thought you had a history paper to write."

"Phooey," Jessica complained. "I got sick of all those kings. Did you know one of them had six wives?"

Nick spluttered, thinking of what it would be like to have six Jessicas running around in his life.

"Anyway, I wrote that dumb paper and I *still* had all evening to kill. I kept thinking of you racing around ridding the world of crime, while I spent my time climbing the walls." He heard her take a deep breath. "Nick, you *promised* I could go on your next assignment. Even Chief Wallace said it was OK. There's no reason why I can't go.

A promise is a promise. I—"

"Jessica," he interrupted with a laugh. "Before you get yourself into a tizz, that's why I'm calling you."

"Oh, Nick!" she squealed. He could hear the springs of her bed creaking and knew she was probably jumping up and down for joy. "A real undercover police assignment! I can't wait!"

"Calm down, Jess," he teased. "I don't think the trustees of SVU will appreciate your breaking their bed."

Jessica giggled and the creaking noise ceased. "OK, I'm ready. Shoot."

Shoot. Nick shuddered, all his pleasure at making her happy suddenly falling away. His eyes traveled to the hallway outside the glass-enclosed bullpen where the detectives sat. A row of handcuffed perpetrators were slumped glumly on a bench waiting for their cases to be processed. Any one of them could have committed his crime with a gun.

Nick glanced at the far wall of the room. There he saw the row of framed citations—memorials to the good cops who'd been struck down in the line of duty. Police work wasn't a joke. It was deadly serious.

"Jess, don't use words like that around a cop, OK?"

She snorted. "Don't be so uptight. I was only kidding."

Nick gripped the handle of the phone. "I mean it. If something were to happen to you while we were on assignment, I would never forgive myself."

"*Nothing* is going to happen to me," Jessica said sweetly. "You'll be there to protect me. Now tell me about our case."

Nick closed his eyes. He still thought this was a bad idea. Jessica had the will, but he was afraid she didn't have the control. She was too fearless. Sometimes he thought she didn't realize his job involved life-and-death danger; it was nothing like the movies.

"Come *on*, Nick," she prompted, as if sensing his reluctance. "I'll be a complete professional."

Nick opened his jade-green eyes and ran a hand through his dark, tousled hair. "OK," he sighed. "But no fooling around. We'll be working undercover as a couple."

"That'll be easy," Jessica assured him. "We already *are* a couple."

Nick laughed. "Brilliant deduction, detective. But listen, let's meet at the corner of Pine and Twelfth in an hour. I'll brief you on the rest of the assignment then."

"I'll be there," she replied gaily.

"Twelve-thirty, Jess. Don't be late."

"Twelve-thirty!" Jessica squealed. "I've gotta book!"

Hearing a sudden click, Nick smiled and put

down the phone. He knew Jessica was heading straight for the mirror. Even though her flawless good looks and killer body turned heads no matter how little effort she put into her appearance, she still loved to go all out, doing up her long, blond hair, dressing to the nines, and making the most of her natural beauty with her expert application of makeup.

She'll pass for a country club girl, no problem, Nick thought. *And that'll make it a hundred times easier for me to blend into the Verona Springs Country Club scene for this assignment.* But if this was such a good idea, why did he feel uneasy?

"Because you love her too much to expose her to danger," he muttered as he thumbed through the files on his desk. That's why he'd decided this would be his last assignment. *As long as I'm working as an undercover cop,* Nick knew, *Jessica's going to keep insisting I take her out on the job.*

He still shuddered when he recalled that chop-shop investigation he'd worked and how she'd followed him down to the stakeout at the docks—despite his warnings not to. It had all worked out in the end, but Jessica easily could have been killed. And despite that experience, Jessica clearly felt that undercover work was all fun and glamour. Maybe this assignment would show her what it was really all about: hours of tedious boredom punctuated by moments of tremendous danger and high anxiety.

"Please, don't let anything bad happen to Jessica," he wished aloud. "And please, let this assignment put her off undercover work for good."

"Hey, Fox," Bill Fagen called over. "You're talking to yourself again. You *sure* you're not losing it?"

Nick shook his head sadly. "This time you may be right, Fagen," he acknowledged with a sigh. "If I'm bringing Jessica Wakefield along on an undercover investigation, I *must* be losing it!"

Chapter Two

"Unbelievable," Tom murmured under his breath as he surveyed the extensive grounds of the Verona Springs Country Club. The reflection of the bright California sun shimmered across the boating pond, and the colorful gardens were lit up in a riot of pinks, reds, golds, and oranges, perfuming the warm, late morning air with the sweet scent of roses and mimosa.

Tom let out an appreciative whistle as he made his way across the golf course in search of the old gardener. He'd realized the place was amazing in the short time he'd spent there yesterday afternoon with Dana Upshaw. Now that he'd had a chance to wander around the palatial clubhouse alone, noting the two Olympic-size pools, clay and grass tennis courts, and this impeccably groomed 18-hole golf course, Tom was in awe.

George sure knows how to say he's sorry, Tom

thought. It was Mr. Conroy who'd sent Tom the two memberships to the country club in the first place. A goodwill gesture or a bribe, Tom wasn't sure.

But it would take more than expensive gifts for Tom to forget the stack of secret photographs he'd found in Mr. Conroy's rolltop desk. Shots of Elizabeth—many taken with a zoom lens—proving he'd been obsessed with her. And proving to Tom once and for all how wrong he'd been not to believe Elizabeth's stories about Mr. Conroy's inappropriate and unwanted advances.

Tom felt a sharp pain in his jaw and gingerly unclenched his teeth. "It's going to take a long time for me to forgive you, George," he vowed. "Perhaps forever."

"Can I help you?"

Tom started at the sound of the low, gravelly voice. He turned to see a beefy man standing before him, his huge forearms roped with muscles. He was dressed in white slacks and a white polo shirt, a putting iron held casually in his left hand.

Tom swallowed. The only person he wanted to speak to was the old gardener. "Um . . . you're the club pro?"

"That's right," the man said, extending his right hand. "Jeff Ryan. Have you lost your party?"

Tom shook his head. "I was just . . ." What *was* he doing out in the middle of the golf course? He couldn't very well say he was admiring the flowers.

"Let's step over here, sir," the pro advised, leading Tom toward a tight clump of trees. "Golf balls can be pretty dangerous."

Tom gulped. Was this man threatening him? He'd better come up with a plausible story—and quick. But not just any story would do. Everyone was suspicious—including the pro. If Tom was caught with an unsupportable alibi, he could be in deep.

"I was looking for the gardener," Tom started. "I . . ." He shoved his hand into the pocket of his chinos and pulled out his pocketknife. "I borrowed this from him to open my glove compartment yesterday. I wanted to return it."

The pro shrugged his bulky shoulders. "Looks like you get to keep it, pal. Old Juan no longer works here."

Tom narrowed his eyes. "Maybe you're thinking of someone else. Like I said, I just saw him yesterday."

The pro smiled lazily and twirled his putting iron. "Is that so?"

Tom felt the muscles in his back tense. If the pro forced him one more step into the grove, they would no longer be visible from the green. And Tom couldn't afford to take any chances. It would be fight or flight—no in-betweens.

But what chance do I have when he's wielding that golf club? Tom wondered desperately. *Slim to none.*

The pro leaned the putting iron against his shoulder nonchalantly. "College boy, aren't you? SVU? You know, we've had some trouble with SVU students around here."

Tom could feel his face burning. He tried to maneuver around the pro, but he was being forced deeper and deeper into the woods.

Suddenly a group of four men in loud checkered pants came strolling into view on the edge of the green.

"Hey, Jeff," one of them yelled. "What's taking so long with my putting iron?"

The pro's smile vanished from his face. He gave Tom one last hooded look and then turned his attention to the men. "It's right here, Mr. Ellson."

Tom watched with relief as the pro stepped away and joined the other golfers. *I'll have to be more careful from now on,* he thought, scrambling onto the green. *Or I might end up in the Verona Springs Reservoir myself!*

"Izzy, you've *got* to help me!" Jessica squealed as she pounded on the door to her friend's dorm suite. "Time is of the essence."

The door flew open immediately. "What is it?" Isabella Ricci cried, her radiant gray eyes as wide as saucers. "Are you in trouble?"

Jessica ran into the living room. "Of the worst kind! I'm finally going to work undercover with

Nick, and I don't have a *thing* to wear." She came to a screeching halt. "I can't believe I just said that, but it's completely true."

Isabella groaned. "You've *got* to be kidding." She pushed the door shut. "I thought something serious had happened."

Jessica collapsed onto Isabella's blue velvet couch. "This *is* serious. I'm supposed to meet Nick in less than forty-five minutes. I need a total transformation, and I don't know where to begin."

"What do you mean 'a total transformation'? What's the assignment?"

Jessica shrugged. "You know what? He never told me. But when Nick's working undercover he always looks so . . . *dangerous.*" She shivered as the image of Nick's hard-bitten good looks came back to her. His jeans always seemed to be ripped in just the right places, his battered leather jacket usually hanging sexily across his broad, muscular shoulders.

"Earth to Jess," Isabella teased. "Where do *I* fit in here? I don't exactly dress like someone on the run from the fashion police. Do I?"

Jessica sat up and stared at her impeccably put-together sorority sister. Today's ensemble was a white linen pantsuit and a gold ribbed top. "No, of course not. But you *did* go as a biker chick for Halloween. . . . I know! Maybe I could borrow those black PVC pants you wore. If I'm supposed to infiltrate the scum of society, they'll probably help a bunch."

"You're right," Isabella said, seeming to get into the swing of things. "With my silver shirt and your denim jacket . . ."

Jessica clapped her hands excitedly and sprung to her feet. "Do you still have those sleazy red dangling earrings? I want to look as cheap as possible."

"Let's take a look," Isabella offered, leading Jessica toward her bedroom.

Jessica quickly threw off her yellow flowered sundress and slipped into Isabella's clothes. The shiny PVC pants were a bit of a struggle, but with a lot of baby powder and elbow grease, she eventually eased them on.

Almost hyperventilating with excitement, Jessica ran to the full-length mirror. Her body looked perfect. The tight silver shirt and low-waisted, black vinyl pants gave her an edgy, streetwise look. But when she met Isabella's eyes in the mirror, they both shook their heads. Jessica's body was saying one thing, but her blond hair and wholesome Californian good looks were saying something else.

Jessica dropped down onto Isabella's bed in despair. "It's hopeless. I'll never pass for a hardened criminal. Nick's going to take one look at me and kick me off the case before I've even been briefed."

Isabella cocked her head. "Wait a minute. I have an idea."

"What?" Jessica mumbled, barely listening.

Isabella suddenly dropped to her knees and began rooting through the bottom of her closet, throwing shoes, squash racquets, and books over her shoulder. "I know I put it here *some*where." She tucked a dark curl behind her ear. "One of my old suitemates left it behind . . ."

Jessica bounced up and tried to peer over her friend's shoulder, careful to avoid any flying objects. "What are you looking for?" she asked, trying not to get her hopes up. They'd been *so* close. What could Isabella possibly have in mind? She had less than ten minutes left if she was going to be on time to meet Nick!

"Voila," Isabella cried, leaping to her feet. In her hand was an oversized can: spray-on hair color of the cheapest kind.

"I couldn't," Jessica gasped, taking a step back. Her hands flew up protectively to her hair.

Isabella shook the can in her hand. "Take your pick. It's either this or good-bye career on the police force."

Jessica groaned and gave one more tender pat to her flowing blond locks. "Spray ahead, Izzy. If this doesn't show Nick I'm serious about undercover work, nothing will!"

"Tom Watts?" a familiar voice inquired.

Tom looked up, startled, from where he'd been sitting at one of the little tables on the flagstone patio at the Verona Springs Country Club. It took him a moment to recognize the statuesque brunette in the lime-green sundress before him.

"Lila! Hello," he finally managed. But the two skinny girls behind her, wearing blindingly bright clothes and matching skeptical looks, were strangers to him.

"Tom Watts, I'd like you to meet Pepper Danforth and Bunny Sterling," Lila introduced. "They're long-time members of the club. *VIPs.*"

Tom stood and offered his hand. "Nice to meet you both." He hoped he wasn't about to get caught up in a long conversation. Before Lila had appeared, he'd been deep in thought about his next move. His reporter's instinct told him there was a cover-up going on. But with the old gardener gone—on the run or maybe worse—he needed time to figure out how he was going to get to the bottom of it.

Bunny squealed, giving his fingers a soft squeeze. "Likewise. You know, you're *so* handsome! Daddy would love you. Do you do movies?"

Tom smiled, looking over at Lila for help.

She raised an eyebrow. *Sorry,* it seemed to say.

"I haven't seen you around here before," Pepper said throatily, her silvery blue eyes practically boring into his. She held his hand for longer than was necessary.

Lila gave Tom a quizzical look. "Um . . . what *does* bring you here, anyway?"

Tom felt his stomach tighten sharply. Everyone at SVU knew Lila came from one of the richest families in Sweet Valley. Maybe *she* was wondering how *he* could afford a membership at Verona Springs too. It seemed as if everyone knew how until recently he'd only been able to attend SVU on a hardship scholarship. *But that's all changed now,* he reminded himself, *since George made me the beneficiary of a trust fund. I wonder if Lila knows that?* Sure, he'd probably never be as rich as the Lila Fowlers and Bruce Patmans of the world, but now he could afford to join the country club even if Mr. Conroy *hadn't* given him the memberships as a gift. "In case you didn't know," he snapped, "my trust fund—"

Lila laughed good-naturedly, cutting him off. "Um, what I meant was, this is the *Couples Only* section of the club. I *know* you and Liz aren't exactly . . . ?"

"A couple," Tom finished for her, his face turning ten shades of red.

"Oooh, does that mean you're free?" Bunny gushed, grabbing hold of his arm.

"If he was *free,*" Pepper hissed, pulling Bunny's hands away, "he wouldn't be *allowed* here, would he? And neither would *you,* I might add. Have you forgotten your fiancé?"

"Oh, right," Bunny replied. "Ooops!"

I'm dead! Tom realized, his heartbeat pounding in his temples. *I need a girlfriend, and I need one fast!* But who? Would Dana even consider talking to him again after the way he'd blown her off to do research on this story yesterday? And if she did, was it fair to keep using her as his cover?

Tom had to admit there was a time when he'd thought he had genuine feelings for Dana, but now he knew he'd just been on the rebound. In truth, he'd been doing practically nothing but leading Dana on. All he could do in his mind was compare her to Elizabeth—failingly.

But Liz is over you, chump, a cruel voice reminded him. *And if you're going to get this story, you're going to need that cover.*

"If you'll excuse me," he announced, getting up from his chair. "I think I hear my girlfriend calling me right now!"

"I don't see the gardener anywhere," Elizabeth complained, shielding her eyes from the bright noon sun. She rummaged through her pocketbook, pulled out her sunglasses, and slipped them on. "We tried the greenhouse and the main garden. I don't know where else to look."

Scott sighed. "There's a watering can by those flowers over there." He pointed to a bed of pink geraniums on the edge of the golf course. "Maybe he stepped away for a minute."

"It's worth a try," Elizabeth mumbled, heading

for the abandoned can. Just then a huge brick of a man in white started crossing the green.

"Excuse me!" Elizabeth called. "Sir!"

"What are you doing?" Scott whispered frantically, clamping his hand on her shoulder. "I thought we'd agreed not to call attention to ourselves."

Elizabeth shook his hand off as the man approached. "Trust me," she whispered back.

"Yes?" the man asked. He wore an emblem with two crossed golf clubs on his polo shirt.

"We're from the *Sweet Valley Gazette*. We were hoping to find someone to talk to about these beautiful geraniums. The newspaper is doing a lifestyle piece on the club and—"

The man smiled, his large white teeth glinting predatorily in the sunlight. "Sorry, miss. I can tell you anything you want about golf, but flowers aren't exactly my specialty."

Elizabeth forced a girlish giggle. "Of *course* not. But maybe you could tell us where the gardener is? I think he's an elderly Latino."

The golf pro's smile faded a notch. "That's right. Old Juan certainly is popular today." Sarcasm colored his voice. "Too bad he's not around anymore. Kind of makes you wonder."

Popular today? Not around anymore? Elizabeth kept her expression as placid as she could despite her pounding heart. "What do you mean?"

The pro indicated the patio with a jut of his

square jaw. "Guy over there on the phone was looking for him too. Says Juan lent him a pocketknife."

Elizabeth looked over toward the patio, her face heating up as she realized the *guy* in question was none other than Tom Watts! She felt her blood boil in anger. *How dare he!* she thought. *He's going to mess everything up, barging into my investigation with his lame stories.*

A pocketknife! How lame. Was Tom trying to bury this story before they'd even started? For both of them to show up and start asking for the gardener was a big mistake. Especially considering that since yesterday, the gentle, sweet gardener seemed to have fled the scene—or had been taken out of the picture entirely. Anyone involved in the cover-up would be put on alert now for sure.

"What else did he want?" Elizabeth cried, unable to stop herself.

The pro narrowed his eyes. "Excuse me?"

Scott gave a nervous laugh and took hold of Elizabeth's arm. "She thinks everyone's from a rival paper." He patted Elizabeth's hand. "I'm sure that young man isn't interested in these lovely geraniums, Liz. Now let's go look at those Louis XIV chairs in the drawing room. I'm sure our editor would love to know about those."

Shamefaced, Elizabeth let herself be led away, knowing how close she'd come to blowing their cover. "I'm sorry, Scott," she mumbled when they were out of earshot. "But hearing that Juan is missing—and knowing that Tom is sticking his nose into *my* story—that *really* makes me see red. We're *all* in jeopardy now."

Scott shrugged. "Don't worry about it. Whatever damage there is has already been done by him. Let's just hope we can get to the right people before he messes us up a second time."

Elizabeth felt her internal temperature gauge heating up all over again. "You're right, Scott. I'm going to read Tom the riot act," she vowed as they headed for the patio. "If he doesn't butt out, we'll all wind up as fish food in the reservoir—which is probably where poor, innocent Juan Mendoza is right now!"

"I'm coming!" Dana shouted to the ringing phone. "Hold on!"

Blast it, she thought, grabbing her hot pink terrycloth robe. *Why does it always have to ring when I'm in the tub and my roommates are out?* She streaked down the hall toward her room, leaving a trail of wet footprints behind her. "Yes?" she said breathlessly when she picked up the receiver.

"Dana? It's Tom."

"Tom," Dana repeated, her heart doing a somersault in her chest. He was the last person she'd expected to hear from. After his brusque behavior yesterday—cutting short their date at the Verona Springs Country Club—she'd been sure she'd lost him for good. Could she have been wrong? A weak, hopeful smile started to play at the edges of her full lips. "How are you?"

"Fine," he said, his tone neutral. "I wanted to apologize for yesterday. Running out on you at the country club before we got to hear the string quartet . . . was . . . rude. I'm sorry."

Dana slipped into her robe and sat down on her bed, listening carefully. The words were right, but she sensed a coolness underneath them. She pushed back a long, wet ringlet of mahogany hair from her forehead and waited for him to go on.

"I mean, I was hoping I could make it up to you. Today, even."

Dana felt the small glimmer of hope inside of her begin to grow. Had Tom finally realized that they really could make a great couple? Or was this just another pull on her heartstrings? Her weeks as Tom's maybe-maybe-not girlfriend had not been easy. They'd been in what felt like a very precarious dance—one step forward, two steps back.

"I don't know," she ventured, cursing herself as the words slipped out. Why was she hesitating? She'd been attracted to Tom since the first time she'd seen him outside his father's condo. Tom's clean, classic features and winning smile had sent her heart into overdrive. But it seemed like every time they started to get close, Tom's past—in the form of his ice-cold ex-girlfriend, Elizabeth Wakefield—managed to pop up and wrench them apart.

Dana shuddered, wrapping her robe tightly around her slender figure as she remembered the love letter Tom had left for Elizabeth at the WSVU station. *The letter I stole,* she thought giddily. *The letter that's tucked away in my jewelry box where Elizabeth will never see it.* If she could just keep them apart long enough, she was sure Tom would eventually begin to love her. She'd almost succeeded once.

"Dana?" Tom's voice cut into her thoughts. "Are you still there?"

"Yes, Tom . . . sorry. I'm just a little surprised to hear your voice."

"I hope you don't mind me calling."

Mind? Dana thought, twisting the belt of her robe. *Is he* that *blind?* "No, I don't mind. Not if you really mean it this time." She winced. She knew better than to push him for greater commitment when he clearly wasn't ready yet. "Um . . . I didn't mean that like it sounded. It's just that I hate getting excited about a concert and then having to miss it." *And we're perfect together,* her mind added. *Can't you see that?*

Tom cleared his throat. "Maybe this isn't such a great idea . . . excuse me, hold on . . . "

Dana felt as if the bottom had dropped out of her world. She bit her lip to keep from crying out, "Don't leave me!"

But then suddenly Tom was back on the line. "Actually, Dana, that's an excellent idea! I'd love to hear the string quartet this afternoon. And it just wouldn't be right if I didn't have you there to fill me in on all the subtleties."

Dana leapt up, a huge smile plastered across her face. "Really, Tom?" Her head was spinning. She thought for sure he had been about to tell her to forget it and hang up.

"I can't wait to see you," he gushed, his voice more affectionate than ever.

"Tom," she cried, her pulse racing. "I can't wait to see you either. And I've got the *best* news. The music director of the Verona Springs Country Club called me this morning. Their cello player is on vacation and they want me to fill in! My instructor, Anthony, recommended me. Can you believe it? I'm playing this afternoon!"

There was a short pause. "Really? That's . . . that's an amazing coincidence. Then again, you're an amazing musician, Dana. You deserve the job more than anyone."

"Tom, you're too sweet." She laid back on her bed and kicked her feet in the air. Had Tom finally seen the light? In the one moment he'd been off the phone, his whole personality seemed to have changed. "Since you're already there at the club and I have to play in a few hours, why don't we meet beforehand for tea?"

"Perfect," Tom agreed warmly. "How soon can you get here?"

As soon as possible, she thought. "Give me . . . an

hour. Two if I can't get my roommate's old Plymouth to start."

"Where should we meet?"

"Well, I have to pick up my sheet music in the employees' lounge first. I can meet you by the gazebo after that."

"Um . . . why don't we just meet outside the employees' lounge?" Tom suggested, his voice suddenly dropping to a whisper.

Dana frowned. Why would Tom want to wait around by the "servants' quarters" when he could relax in the fresh air of the club's lovely gazebo? *Because he's dying to see you!* she thought, her heart thudding with pleasure.

"It'll be easier for you," Tom added, almost on cue. "Besides, if I'm going to have to turn you over to the string quartet, I'll want to spend as much time with you as possible first."

Dana grinned so wide she thought her face would crack. "OK! I'll get there as soon as I can."

"I'll be counting the minutes." Tom laughed.

Dana hung up the phone and jumped up on her bed. "Yeah!" she screamed, bouncing up and down in the air. "Move over, Elizabeth Wakefield. Tom Watts is *mine* now!"

Chapter Three

"I'll be counting the minutes, Dana," Tom repeated to the dial tone that had clicked in after Dana hung up. "Yeah. You too. Bye now." He affected a chuckle before replacing the phone on the hook and turning to acknowledge the hostile glare of his ex-girlfriend.

I hope you heard every word, Liz, he thought viciously. He'd known Elizabeth was there from the moment she'd stepped onto the patio, her aquamarine eyes burning two hot holes into his back.

He'd almost dropped the phone during his call to Dana when he first saw her and Scott Sinclair striding toward him, their two blond heads bent close together. It was out of sheer spite that he'd decided to launch into his Romeo routine with Dana. "Yes, Elizabeth?" he asked smugly, crossing his arms over his light blue polo shirt. "Is there something I can do for you?"

Elizabeth's eyes narrowed angrily. "Absolutely! You can clear out. This is *our* story."

"Oh, so it's *both* of yours now, I take it," Tom shot back, even more glad of the little show he'd put on. Elizabeth was practically throwing her new relationship with that loser Sinclair in his face. "Since when do stories have a limit on reporters?"

Elizabeth stamped her sandaled foot. "Since your meddling might be putting us all in danger. Scott and I can't find that old gardener anywhere. Who knows what might have happened to him? Whoever is behind this whole thing *knows* we're on to them, Tom. And I want you to stay out of our way before you mess everything up again."

Tom felt hot color flushing his cheeks. "That won't be hard to do, since I'm way ahead of you two. If anyone's going to mess this story up, it's *you.*" He jabbed his finger at her. "Why don't you and Sinclair find a new piece to work on and leave the hard stuff to the *real* reporters?"

"You make me *sick,*" Elizabeth hissed, taking a step back. "You think this is a joke, flirting with your—your *girlfriend* when people's lives are at stake!"

Tom flinched when he saw the pain flicker in her eyes. Immediately he wished he could take it all back, especially the performance he put on with Dana. Suddenly he wanted to cradle Elizabeth in his arms and tell her how much he still loved her.

How much he still cared. How she was the one he'd always loved.

"Liz . . . ," he started, taking a step toward her. But suddenly Scott draped his arm protectively around her shoulder. Tom felt his words and his feelings of longing dry like bitter pellets in his mouth.

"Don't listen to Mr. Telegenic," Scott sneered. "He'll get a couple of sound bites and think he's the man."

Tom clenched his fists and for a moment saw scarlet. "Don't count on it, Sinclair. Or you either, Elizabeth. I'm running circles around you on this story." His skull throbbed in anger and frustration as he stalked off toward the employees' lounge. "I'm warning you—be careful, or you'll choke on my dust!"

"Where *are* you, Nick?" Jessica murmured. She bent down and peered through the grimy window of the old pawn shop. The big clock hanging over the cash register read 12:35. Despite her last minute preparations, she'd been on time practically to the second. But where was Nick?

Jessica gnawed on her bottom lip and looked around. Pine and Twelfth wasn't exactly the Rodeo Drive of Sweet Valley. Across the street was an off-track betting parlor with several unsavory-looking characters hanging around outside. Next to the pawn shop was a boarded-up liquor store.

"Get used to it, Jess," she told herself. "No

more fancy places for you. If you're going undercover, then this is your life from now on."

Jessica groaned jealously as she imagined herself sipping iced tea at the poolside patio of the Verona Springs Country Club. Sure, she'd never been there, but Lila had told her plenty. She felt like she knew the place, even though she was certain she'd never actually *go* there now.

"Not if I'm going to stay in character," she scolded herself. "And anyway, who needs country clubs and fancy restaurants? In this new life, I'll be having a thrill a minute."

But when is that minute going to start? she wondered anxiously. *And what in the world is holding Nick up?* Jessica felt herself begin to get seriously creeped out. "Maybe I have the address wrong," she mumbled, her nerves starting to prick at the edges of her consciousness. She rummaged through her beaten-up leather bag until she found the hastily scrawled slip of paper. Pine and Twelfth, it read.

"But is this Twelfth?" she wondered. The street sign was bent and covered with graffiti—impossible to make out. "Well, the one before it was Eleventh, so this must be Twelfth."

Or 10th! she realized with a start. She felt her heart start to pound. *Have I been standing on the wrong corner this whole time?*

Suddenly the doors of the betting parlor flew open and three seedy looking men spilled out onto the sidewalk. A souped-up low-rider blew past, sending torn up betting slips flitting across the road where they joined other scraps of garbage in the gutter.

"It was fixed!" one of the men complained in a gravelly voice. A huge smoldering cigar dangled from the corner of his mouth. "Blue Stallion was a sure thing in the sixth. I got a mind to call up the commissioner."

"Give it a rest, Moe," his friend in a faded blue work shirt sneered. "You're always saying the races are fixed."

"Yeah? Well that one was!"

"Excuse me," Jessica called. "Sorry to bother you, uh, *gentlemen,* but could you tell me what street this is?"

"Gentlemen?" The man named Moe looked up and plucked the cigar from his mouth. "Hey, sweetheart, it's the Avenue of Broken Dreams. Want to mend mine?"

The other men around him laughed. Then, to her chagrin, they began heading across the street toward her.

"Very funny," Jessica said. "But I'm serious. Is this Tenth or Twelfth Street?"

Moe placed his hands over his heart. "Baby," he began as he approached her, "for you, I'll make it anything you want."

Jessica pressed her lips tightly together. This was getting her nowhere, except into the middle of a lot of unwanted attention. *Not* the best position for an undercover operative.

"Moe, give the kid a break," the man in the faded shirt said. "It's Twelfth Street, lady."

"But hey," Moe persisted, "do you want some company?"

"No!" Jessica fumed, glaring at the group of men. "As soon as my boyfriend gets here—"

"Boyfriend?" Moe interrupted. "What, does he handle your business for you?"

How did he know that? she wondered, her stomach sinking. *Oh no—He can tell I'm working undercover, and now he knows my boyfriend's a cop! My career is over before it's even getting started!*

"Aw, come on." Moe took another step forward, making Jessica back up against the wall. "Don't look so shocked. I know what you've got going, honey."

"Really?" Jessica squeaked. *Nick oh Nick oh Nick oh Nick please hurry up and get here!* she pleaded silently, no longer caring if he saw her blow her one chance at the big time.

"Yeah, really." Moe chortled, displaying some unsightly brown flecks between his teeth and roasting her with dragon breath. "Now, your boyfriend . . . he handles the money end of things, right?"

"Money?" Jessica wondered aloud. As the word hung in the air, it all became clear. "You think I'm a . . . of all the crazy . . . I'm *not* that kind of girl!"

Moe rocked back and laughed, his buddies joining in. "Hard to get, eh? Well, why don't you just run home, little girl, if you can't take care of business for yourself."

Jessica turned away, her face reddening and her brows knitting together in fury. *Is this some kind of test?* she wondered angrily. *What, does Nick think I'm only suited to work on the* Vice Squad? *How* insulting! *If he thinks I'm going to settle for this, he's got another thing coming!*

Jessica threw her hands to her hips. She was just about to give the pack of losers a piece of her mind when she heard footsteps behind her. She whipped around, Nick's name on her lips. But instead of her rough and ready boyfriend, a pathetic-looking nerd with greasy hair and thick horn-rims went lumbering past. *Some help he'd be,* Jessica thought. *Who knows? He's probably some powerful, dangerous drug dealer. No cop would ever believe he's capable of doing anything more illegal than computer hacking.*

"Hey, Poindexter!" Moe called out amid puffs of cigar smoke. "Lose your compass?"

The other men fell against each other, hooting. Jessica broke into a grin herself until she noticed that the nerd had clenched his fists. Even though he was wearing a short-sleeve, button-down shirt and too-tight, too-short chinos, she could see that his arms were incredibly muscular. *What a neighborhood!* she thought. *Even the geeks look like they can rip you from limb to limb.*

Jessica guessed the creeps must have noticed too, because suddenly, without another word, they were all jogging back across the street toward the betting parlor. Jessica sighed. *At least those jerks finally left me alone,* she thought. *But where on Earth is Nick?*

"I'm OK, Scott," Elizabeth said, feeling a twinge of annoyance as Tom disappeared from view. "You can let go of me now."

"Oh—OK." Scott removed his hand and tugged on the sleeve of his shirt. "Sorry, but we *are* on country club grounds, you know. I didn't want anyone to see me let you get attacked by some jerk who happens to be your ex-boyfriend." He cleared his throat. "And besides . . . I thought you could use the backup."

Elizabeth sighed. "Thanks for coming to the rescue. But I'm capable of fighting my own battles—"

"Hey, look!" Scott exclaimed, cutting her off. "Isn't that . . . what's her name . . . Lila Fowler? Heading toward the clubhouse?"

Elizabeth looked up and sure enough there was Lila, wearing a short, lime-green sundress, disappearing into the club's stately main building.

Scott grabbed Elizabeth's hand and started to pull her across the terrace.

"Where are we going?" Elizabeth cried, her long, blue skirt catching on a loose piece of rattan that was jutting from one of the deck chairs. "Wait!"

Scott stopped, his blue eyes turning on like thousand-watt klieg lights. "When we got here, I overheard someone say that a woman named Lila was organizing the club tennis tournament. Maybe it's her! If we sign up to compete, it'll give us the perfect cover for our investigation."

"Well, we're not actual members," Elizabeth pointed out as she unhooked her skirt from the chair and followed after him. "But I bet Lila can pull some strings for us."

I've got to admit, that's a great idea, she thought. *Besides, our editor asked us to write about the tournament in the first place. Let's see Tom come up with a better cover than that!*

"Lila!" Elizabeth called as they caught up to her just inside the spacious clubhouse.

Lila turned. "Elizabeth! What are you doing here?" She gave a curious glance toward Scott.

"This is Scott Sinclair," Elizabeth announced, a little out of breath. "He's helping me with a piece on the mixed doubles tennis tournament for the *Sweet Valley Gazette.*"

Scott smiled. "We heard you're organizing the tournament. That's quite an honor. But from everything I've heard about you, you certainly deserve it."

Lila giggled and smoothed back a strand of her silky brown hair, obviously pleased. "Yes, thank you. But I was a bit surprised myself."

Scott chuckled, moving over to a large leather

sofa and offering her a seat. "Oh, don't be modest. Everyone at SVU knows what a great job you did with Lila's Doughnuts. The club is lucky to have you."

Elizabeth stifled a groan as she trailed behind them. If her memory served her right, Lila's first business venture had been almost a total disaster. Scott sure was laying it on thick. But from the way Lila's brown eyes were sparkling, she guessed he knew his audience.

"Oh, thank you . . . Scott, was it?" She beamed as she took a seat. "You're much too kind."

Scott sat down beside Lila and motioned for Elizabeth to join them. "Not at all. Actually Elizabeth was just saying what an excellent slant it would give our story if we could actually *play* in the tournament."

Elizabeth remained standing, as the brightness in Lila's eyes dimmed a notch.

Lila looked down at her lap. "I don't know about that. I already have a pretty full roster . . . plus you're *not* members."

Scott ignored her comment. "We're planning two side-by-side pieces, one about the difficult behind-the-scenes job of organizing the tournament. Naturally, *you'll* feature *very* prominently." He paused for a moment, Elizabeth could tell, to let his heavy schmooze sink in. "The part about us playing in the tournament would be tiny. What we call a *sidebar* in the journalism trade. But the problem is that without the participation angle, our editor might not take the main story."

As she watched the conflicting emotions on Lila's face, Elizabeth had to hand it to Scott. He really *did* know how to pull the right strings.

Lila sighed. "I think it's a great idea. I really do. It's just that the tournament is for couples, not writing partners."

"Oh," Scott laughed, jumping up and throwing his arm clumsily around Elizabeth. "Is that all you're worried about? I thought you knew—we *are* a couple."

"Oh! Well, in *that* case," Lila smiled, rising quickly to her feet. "I'll get you a sign-up sheet. And please let me know when the photographers arrive. I'll be *glad* to pose for *any* and *all* pictures!"

Elizabeth knocked Scott's arm off her shoulder as soon as Lila walked away. "That was awfully underhanded, Scott. Word is going to get around—"

"So what?" he said innocently. "Is that so bad? I thought we agreed we'd play it as a couple. If I hadn't told her that, we wouldn't be in the tournament, now, would we?"

"I guess not," Elizabeth muttered. *But you'd better remember this is only make-believe,* she added silently.

"Bruce, guess what?" Lila called, spying her boyfriend in his bright tennis whites standing by the pool bar.

Bruce turned, his twinkling blue eyes reflecting the crystal clear pool water. "We've won the lottery?"

Lila kissed him lightly on the cheek. "Don't be silly. Why would I get excited about that? This is important news."

Bruce laughed. "Lila Fowler, you're one of the few people I know who can afford to turn her nose up at the thought of winning the lottery." He gestured toward the bar. "Do you want anything?"

Lila peered at his drink. It was a frothy concoction of orange, yellow, and green that smelled vaguely like citrus. "What is that?"

Bruce plucked out the little red umbrella. "It's a banana smoothie with papaya juice and two limes thrown in for good measure."

Lila took a sip, the three flavors exploding on her taste buds. "Delicious! Oh, I'll have one of those, please."

The bartender turned to whip up the ingredients in his blender.

Lila handed Bruce his drink. "Now let me tell you the news! I just signed up Elizabeth and her new boyfriend, Scott, for the tournament."

"Really?" Bruce gave her a skeptical look. "Is that smart? I don't think Liz is even a member of the Verona Springs Country Club. I thought you were just going after people with prestige."

Lila frowned and crossed her slender arms.

"Well, it's true Liz isn't exactly *rich*, but she *is* a major personality at SVU."

Bruce finished off his smoothie and placed the glass on the polished wooden counter. "That's true. But so is Winston Egbert. Would you want *him* playing among the VIPs?"

Lila laughed, imagining Winston tripping over his high-tops as he lunged for a tennis ball in a typically comic faux pas. "This is different. Elizabeth would *never* do anything to embarrass us. Anyway, she and Scott are writing a story about the tournament. And guess who's going to be front page news?"

"Oh, *now* I get it," Bruce scoffed. "You think this will make you some kind of star."

The bartender returned and handed Lila her drink.

"Thank you," she said kindly, before turning her attention to Bruce. "No I don't," she pouted. "I was only thinking of the club. Liz and Scott's story will mean great publicity. How can that be bad?" *My becoming a celebrity will simply be the icing on the cake*, she assured herself.

Bruce held a finger to his lips to indicate silence and, taking her elbow, led her toward a secluded area near the deep end of the pool. "Have you forgotten that Liz is an *investigative* reporter?" he asked in a low voice. "You know the kinds of stories she reports. What if she digs up some dirt or exposes something?"

Lila sat down in a chaise lounge and took a sip of her drink. She hadn't thought about that. "What dirt could there be?" she asked. "All I'm doing is organizing a bunch of tennis matches."

"Hmmm," Bruce murmured, sitting down next to her. He pulled out a pair of Ray Ban sunglasses from the pocket of his shirt and slipped them on. "I don't know."

"Bruce, come on, you're making me nervous," Lila complained. "I thought you'd be pleased. This story's going to reflect well on the club and, most of all, on *us*. We'll be practically *guaranteed* an entree into the ultra-exclusive ranks of Verona Springs."

Bruce flipped up the collar of his shirt. "I guess. But in my experience, reporters have a funny way of finding things out. Especially things their subjects didn't know were there."

Lila sighed and brushed her hair back from her shoulder. "That's *not* going to happen here. *I'm* going to run this tournament strictly by the book. And *I* plan to come off smelling like a rose, no matter what it takes."

Chapter Four

"Typical Jessica behavior," Nick muttered under his breath, rolling his head to unclench the muscles in his neck. "She hounds me to include her in an undercover operation and then blows the simplest part—showing up on time for her briefing."

Nick squinted up and down the street through the thick glasses he was wearing for any sign of Jessica's long, blond hair. He glanced at his watch—12:45. She was now officially fifteen minutes late.

Nick groaned and leaned against the facade of the off-track betting parlor on the corner of Pine and 12th. "How can Jessica expect me to take her seriously as a potential undercover partner if she thinks it's OK to be fashionably late to a vital meeting?"

I can't, he thought. Undercover partners need to have confidence in one another. But he'd known this was a bad idea from the beginning. When Jessica looked at undercover work, she saw only glamour and new-outfit potential. *Maybe her failing to show up isn't so bad after all,* he thought, feeling his anxiety lighten slightly. *It gives me the perfect excuse to kick her off the case. My overprotectiveness doesn't have to come into it.*

Nick looked around again. Now that he'd made up his mind not to work with Jessica, how much longer should he wait? He'd hate to leave and then have her come rushing up, all out of breath with a hundred excuses and no one to explain them to.

Though it *might* serve her right.

He shoved his hands into the pockets of his chinos, which wasn't easy to do, since they were admittedly a bit on the tight side. So what if he hadn't worn them since he was a freshman in high school? They were the only clean pants he was able to find that weren't made out of well-worn black or blue denim.

Ever since those cigar-chomping clowns had piled back into the betting parlor, the sidewalks were empty. All except for a saucily-dressed woman, her hair a bizarre, streaky jet black. She was loitering on the pavement across the street. The overwhelming scent of her cheap perfume was almost making him choke at fifty paces.

What was she up to? Nick wondered, glancing over at her. From the way she was tarting around, he was sure it was no good. He did a quick search through his memory. The woman looked awfully familiar, but he couldn't quite place her.

I know, he thought. *I arrested her for shoplifting a couple of years ago.* No, that wasn't it. He took another look, pushing the glasses down his nose for a better view. *Maybe she was in on that spate of burglaries I worked on last fall.*

All of a sudden it hit him. "That's Nancy Daryl," he whispered to himself. Despite the cool breeze, Nick felt a trickle of sweat break out across his brow. If he was right, the woman standing not twelve feet away was very likely armed and dangerous. *But am I right?* he wondered, throwing another look in the woman's direction.

Huge, dark sunglasses were covering up most of her face. He couldn't risk staring at her. Otherwise she might get skittish and make a run for it—or worse . . .

He caught the woman looking over at him and dropped his eyes. Nancy Daryl's story quickly came back to him. She had a rap sheet that could wallpaper Jessica's dorm room. She'd been in and out of jail for robbery and aggravated assault since the age of sixteen. After her last trial—this one for running a sophisticated con game that had preyed upon senior citizens—she'd threatened to "take care of" each one of the undercover officers who had nailed her; Nick especially. Had she escaped from jail? And if so, why hadn't Chief Wallace warned him?

With a shaky hand, Nick took a handkerchief from his pocket and wiped it across his forehead, thankful for his disguise. The only reason he was still in one piece was because she obviously couldn't place him. *But what happens when Jessica gets here?* he wondered with a start. *Knowing her, she'll scream out my name before she's halfway down the sidewalk.*

Then it'll be curtains for you, copper, he resolved darkly, remembering the chilling baritone of Daryl's voice that day in the courtroom. But what was his alternative? If he left, Jessica might have to face the woman alone. Jessica might approach Daryl and ask if she'd seen Nick, describing him to a *T*. And then *Jessica* would wind up on the receiving end of Daryl's wrath.

Nick felt his stomach go slightly sick at the thought of Jessica coming face to face with a hardened criminal like Daryl. He looked up and down the empty street once more, his heart thudding in his chest. *Stay away, Jessica,* he thought. *Whatever you do, don't show up now!*

"Ah. This is the life for me," Bruce murmured, linking his hands behind his head for optimal lounging comfort. Moments before he'd waved good-bye to Lila, his feeling of relief growing stronger as she darted off in pursuit of more couples for the mixed doubles charity tennis tournament.

"I couldn't be happier about Lila being asked to organize it," he told himself. "But . . ." But, he had to admit, her agitation and anxiety over the event had been putting a major crimp in his quest for total relaxation. He stretched and shifted his weight, luxuriating in the well-padded feel of the chaise lounge. "I think a nap might be in order."

He'd just closed his eyes when the shrill voice of Bunny Sterling snapped them back open.

"Bruuuce!" Bunny gushed. Her large mouth and big, white teeth seemed to hover over him. "You're looking a little chubby these days." She grabbed at his washboard stomach through his white polo shirt, managing to pinch the one spare micro-inch he had.

"Ow," he hollered, sitting up.

Bunny tittered as she smoothed down the skirt of her horrendously ugly minidress. "Oh, you always were *such* a baby. My fiancé, Paul Krandall, wouldn't even have *felt* that. But *he* wouldn't have had any extra fat to pinch in the *first* place."

"Nice to see you too," Bruce retorted.

Bunny smirked. "You always *did* have a sense of humor. But then Daddy always says men use humor to cover up their inadequacies. Which I guess makes you one of the funniest men around."

Bruce gritted his teeth, feeling his head start to throb. He longed to tell Bunny off in the worst way, but he knew that if he did, Lila would skin him alive. He bit his lip and held his tongue, smiling all the while.

"My fiancé, Paul, doesn't have a sense of humor," Bunny continued in her grating voice. "He wouldn't be caught *dead* telling a joke. But then, of course, he doesn't *need* to. He doesn't *have* any inadequacies. Oh look, there he is now!"

Bunny leapt up and started frantically waving to a goofy looking guy who seemed to be wandering aimlessly around the patio. His white tennis top was sloppily tucked into a pair of huge madras shorts that looked as if they were threatening to fall off him at any second.

The guy saw Bunny and waved back, knocking two glasses off a waiter's tray. He then dropped down to his knees, accidentally scattering ice and soda all over the people sitting nearby.

Bunny sat back down with a bright smile. "He'll be here in a minute."

Bruce stifled a laugh. "So, what line of work is your fiancé in?" *Demolition?* he added silently.

Bunny's thick eyebrows rose in surprise. "*Work?* Why, Paul doesn't *work*. He doesn't do *anything!*" she squealed. "His family is *fabulously* wealthy. His father is Sweet Valley's number one congressman. When his father retires, Paul will take over for him."

Bruce made a face. "This is America, Bunny. You don't inherit seats in government. You have to be *elected*."

Bunny threw back a lock of her mousy brown hair, her skinny frame shaking with laughter. "Of course, Bruce," she guffawed. "But who's good enough to oppose him? *You*, maybe?" She held her sides. "Compared to him, you're a big *nothing*."

Bruce clenched his jaw. "Oh really? We Patmans have been holding positions of power since the Pilgrims landed in Massachusetts!"

Bunny brushed a few tears of mirth from her eyes. "What do a bunch of Pilgrims know—except a turkey when they see one?" She jumped to her feet again. "Paul! Paul, sweetie! Over here!"

Paul Krandall came lumbering along the deck of the pool. Just as he was about to reach them, he tripped and crashed over a deck chair, tumbling into Bunny and sending them both sprawling onto Bruce.

Bruce grunted at the impact of Paul's fist in his gut.

"Sorry, old man," Paul stammered, untangling himself from Bunny and standing up. "That water can make these decks a little rocky. I don't have my sea legs yet."

Bruce looked at the motionless deck and frowned. "We're on solid ground here, in case you didn't notice."

"Huh?" Paul asked, scratching the top of his blond head. "You're right. I guess I'd better get new glasses."

"Sweetheart," Bunny said. "You don't *wear* glasses."

Paul's mouth dropped open. "I *don't*? Then why did those kids say I'd dropped them?"

Bunny giggled uneasily. "It was a *joke,* honey. They wanted to see if you'd look down."

Paul scratched his head again. "Oh. No wonder I couldn't find them. I looked for over an hour."

Bunny turned to Bruce with a smug expression on her face. "See? I told you Paul's *far* too superior to require a sense of humor."

Bruce almost fell out of his chair. Sense of humor? This guy wouldn't know a joke if it came up and bit him. In a single, short minute, Paul had proved himself to be by far the stupidest and clumsiest person Bruce had ever met. And while Bunny was no big catch—he knew that all too well—Bruce still couldn't swallow the notion of Bunny preferring *this* geek to a picture of perfection like himself.

Bruce felt indignation bubbling in his stomach. *I can't let her keep believing that Paul's a better man than me,* his ego roared. *I'm suave, sophisticated, and handsome. And this bozo can't even walk without tripping! I'll show them both who's the superior guy. Nobody can prefer a doofus like Krandall to a Patman and get away with it!*

"Oh, good, Lila, I see you're hard at work," Pepper said, her voice thick with syrupy sweetness. She slid into the leather seat next to Lila's at the large mahogany table in the country club's library. "I hope you're not finding this too difficult."

Lila looked up and blinked. *Difficult?* she thought. *It's easy.* All she'd had to do was transfer the names from the sign-up sheets to the playing schedule. "Not at *all,* Pepper. I'm almost finished." She swept her hand around the polished table to indicate the pile of sign-up sheets, her two pads of paper, and the elaborate diagram she'd constructed.

Pepper smiled and smoothed down the pleat in her short tennis skirt. "I'm glad to hear that. Margaret, the woman who had this job before you, botched it up *terribly.* She just didn't understand the rules." Pepper pulled one of Lila's pads of paper toward her. "Oh, look, you *must* have made a mistake. Sharon and Thoreau are paired with Ralph and Lois in the first round."

Lila frowned. "So?"

Pepper gave her a playful push. "What a joker! *Everyone knows* Sharon and Thoreau are the better players. Ralph and Lois wouldn't stand a chance."

Lila frowned again. "But someone has to lose . . . don't they?"

Pepper threw her head back and laughed. "You're such a card." She shook her finger in a mock reprimand. "That sense of humor is going to get you in trouble someday!"

Lila felt her head begin to spin. "I'm sorry. Am I missing something here?"

Pepper's smile immediately vanished as she fixed Lila with her cold, blue eyes. "I hope not. I'd *hate* to have to replace *you* as well. But in case you're feeling a little slow at the moment, let me spell it out for you. People like Ralph and Lois *don't lose* to people like Sharon and Thoreau—understand?"

Lila swallowed, suddenly feeling the dark, paneled walls of the library closing in on her. "You mean the pairings aren't assigned randomly?"

Pepper smirked, running a hand through her tangle of impeccably sprayed and teased hair. "Now *how* could we *possibly* predict the outcome if things were random?"

Lila felt her heart start to pound and she licked her lips nervously. "You mean . . . you want the tournament fixed."

"Fixed?" Pepper asked, raising an eyebrow in mock innocence. "I wouldn't use *that* kind of language. Let's just say a little helping hand never hurts. It makes for a much happier group. And since the group expects the outcome to reflect the social superiority of each couple, why disappoint them?"

Oh, no, Lila thought, stifling a groan. *Bruce was right. Once Elizabeth realizes the tournament's fixed, I'm going to make front page news—as a crook and a scam artist!*

Pepper flicked an imaginary piece of lint from her electric green top. "So like I said before, Lila, this *isn't* proving too difficult for you, is it? Because this tournament can either reflect well on you and Bruce or . . ." Her thin lips spread into a cruel smile. "Well, let's just say *persona non grata* is *not* a title I'd aspire to."

She stood up and started for the door. "Oh, one more thing—and this is *such* a funny story." Pepper let out a small tinkle of false laughter. "That woman I was telling you about, Margaret, the social leper? We got rid of her because she *actually* had the *gall* to pair Bunny and Paul with a former Wimbledon champion and her boyfriend. Can you imagine? Bunny and Paul might have actually *lost!* And *everyone knows* Bunny and Paul win this tournament *every* year." Pepper fell into a fit of giggles before slipping out the door.

But how can I guarantee Bunny and Paul will win? Lila thought dejectedly. *I know! If Bruce and I play against Bunny and Paul, I can control the outcome. All I have to do is make sure they win . . . and that Elizabeth doesn't catch on!*

"I said lime, you imbecile! Not lemon!"

Elizabeth watched in shock as Pepper Danforth flung the contents of her iced tea onto the floor of the club patio. "Bring me a new drink on the double!"

Pepper shoved the now empty glass at the startled young waiter, who took it and headed back toward the kitchen without a second look.

"Now now, Pepper." Bunny laughed and

passed her friend a basket of rolls. "You *know* how the club feels about members abusing the servants."

Pepper grinned wickedly. "I don't see why *we* should have to suffer because none of *them* can speak proper English!"

Elizabeth cringed as the two girls tittered over their fresh fruit plates. She'd noticed that most of the Verona Springs Country Club's staff members were Latino, probably from Mexico or Central and South America. When she thought about hard-working immigrants being treated like second-class citizens by the likes of Pepper Danforth and Bunny Sterling, it made her blind with rage. And this was already the second or third instance of such behavior she'd seen at the club!

Elizabeth's blue-green eyes traveled over the chattering groups on the patio as the next course of the day's luncheon began to be served.

"Hey, *chico,*" a young man in a stylish blue blazer called to a different waiter. "Get me a lemonade." The waiter scurried off. To some, the young man's order might not have sounded unpleasant. But Elizabeth knew that *Chico* was most likely not the waiter's name. *Chico* was Spanish for boy—hardly a term of respect.

Elizabeth pushed her plate of salad away in disgust. *This anger over the treatment of the staff is getting me nowhere,* she thought bleakly. Until she and Scott finished their investigation, her hands were tied. But she vowed to make her next piece an exposé of the awful behavior of certain members of the club. *No one should have to put up with this kind of behavior—I don't care* how *exclusive this place is!*

"Scott," she muttered, standing up. "I'm going to take a walk around."

Scott looked up at her frowning. "But *darling*," he began loudly, "you've barely touched your salad. Do you want me to order you something else?"

Elizabeth shook her head. "I'm not very hungry." Sitting with *this* crowd, she'd be lucky to ever find her appetite again.

"Wait." Scott started to push his chair back. "I'll go with you."

"No," Elizabeth blurted, putting a firm hand on his broad shoulder to keep him down. "I won't be long. You finish your lunch. I'll be back soon."

Elizabeth gave an internal sigh of relief as Scott drew his chair back up to the table. The last thing she needed was Scott trailing after her, acting like an overeager boyfriend, when she needed to sort out her thoughts.

"If you need me, I'll be here, sweetheart," he called, waving his napkin at her.

She forced a smile and ducked around the side of the clubhouse. This time her sigh was loud and clear.

Now, where to start, she thought. *What would*

Tom do? Elizabeth bit her lip. *Tom.* The thought had come quickly and unbidden. She knew he was on the grounds somewhere, trying to scoop her.

"Be honest with yourself, Liz," she murmured. "Your curiosity over his whereabouts has little to do with the story." For a split second during their confrontation by the phone, she'd seen something in his brown eyes. Something she hadn't seen in a very long time—tenderness. If she bumped into him—without Scott—maybe she would see it again.

Elizabeth tightened her ponytail with a rough yank. "Don't be silly," she muttered. "If Tom really cared about me, he'd say something. That look in his eyes was probably a trick of the sunlight."

She shook all thoughts of Tom from her head and marched toward the greenhouse. Maybe one of the other employees could tell her what *really* went on the night Dwayne Mendoza drowned.

The greenhouse was a huge glass building set off to the left of the clubhouse. Elizabeth reached the entrance and hesitated. Were those voices she heard inside?

"Hello," Elizabeth called, stepping into the hot, muggy air of the enclosed space. All around her were rows and rows of large ferns, fragrant orchids, lilac bushes, and crawling vines. The pungent air laid heavily in her lungs and she found breathing difficult.

Even though the greenhouse walls were made of glass, they were steamed up from the moisture within, refracting the afternoon light in an eerie, almost ghostly way. Elizabeth had only gone a few yards when the door behind her flew closed. She gasped and turned, running toward it. She tried to open it, but it was stuck, swollen closed from the almost tropical heat inside.

There must be another way out! she thought, trying to quell the panic in her heart. She started down the nearest aisle, bushy plants brushing against her bare arms. She jumped as one tickled the back of her neck. Whipping around to see who was there, she found a long tendril of ivy that had wormed its way under her collar. "Is anyone in here?" she tried again, only now her voice was a low croak.

Suddenly Elizabeth heard a soft crunch of gravel—*footsteps.* Were they coming toward her or going away? It was impossible to tell with the warped acoustics in the greenhouse. She opened her mouth, but nothing came out. Cold, terrified sweat broke out across her forehead.

Wait a minute! Now the footsteps were right behind her. Was there more than one person? Were they coming at her from both sides?

She spun around and around, frantically searching the aisles for the source of the sound. Out of the corner of her eye she saw something dark streak past her line of vision and disappear behind the ferns. She froze, her heart pounding so hard in her chest that she thought it might explode.

Suddenly a hand reached out as if from nowhere and grasped her shoulder. A silent scream tore through her body before darkness took over.

Chapter Five

"Oh, Liz, I'll get you out of here," Tom murmured. He stared down at the delicate features of his ex-girlfriend, who lay crumpled in his arms. He lifted her gently, cradling her slender body against his chest as he carried her out of the steamy greenhouse. The air outside felt ten times cooler.

Tom dropped to his knees on the grassy knoll beyond the greenhouse door and carefully set Elizabeth down. Her face looked pale; her usual healthy glow had vanished. "C'mon, Liz," he whispered. "C'mon."

Slowly Elizabeth's eyes opened. "What . . . what happened?" She tried to sit up.

"Easy," Tom cautioned. "You fainted." He wrapped a protective arm around her trembling shoulder. "Wait until you catch your breath."

Elizabeth blinked. "I heard someone in the greenhouse. I called out. But they didn't answer." She buried her head in her hands. "I was so frightened."

"It's OK, Liz," he said soothingly. "You're safe. I'd never let anything happen to you."

She looked up at him and for a long powerful moment their eyes seemed locked together. Tom could feel his heart pounding as he leaned ever so slightly toward her. She didn't pull back, instead tilting her head toward his until their lips were no more than a breath apart.

"Hey! Get your hands off my girlfriend!" shouted a voice.

"What?" Tom gasped, twisting around to find Scott Sinclair glowering down at him.

"That's right, Watts!" Scott reached out a hand and pulled Elizabeth to her feet. "You'd better stop bothering her *now.*" He took a menacing step toward Tom.

His brief, beautiful moment with Elizabeth smashed, Tom leapt up, his fists clenched. "Don't worry, Sinclair. She's *all yours!*"

"Listen!" Elizabeth jumped between them, still looking a bit woozy. "Tom rescued me in the greenhouse," she explained in a rush. "Somebody was playing a game of cat and mouse with me and I fainted. But whoever it was might know something important."

"Did you get a good look at him?" Scott asked Tom, his voice still tense.

"Yes, Tom," Elizabeth pressed. "Can you describe him?"

Tom flinched, feeling as if the air had suddenly blown out of his sails. "I . . . um . . . actually . . ." He moistened his lips and tried again. "I think it was me you heard."

"You?" Elizabeth cried, her eyes flashing. "Then why didn't you *answer* me? Why did you creep up behind me and scare me half out of my wits!"

Because I was afraid you were with Sinclair, he answered silently, noting the rising color in her cheeks. *And with good reason.* "I thought . . . you weren't alone."

Elizabeth tossed back her ponytail angrily. "Oh, *I* get it. You thought I might be *interviewing* someone. You were planning to sneak around between the plants and listen in, is that it?"

"No, Liz," Tom protested. "I . . ." He trailed off, defeated. How could Elizabeth believe he would stoop to eavesdropping in order to get a story? *But I can't tell her the truth now,* he thought. *I can't tell her about how much I wanted to take her in my arms after making that call to Dana. Not in front of Sinclair.*

"Well let me tell you something, Tom," Elizabeth continued. "Coming to *my* rescue after *you* caused the crisis doesn't make you a hero in my book!" She grabbed Scott's arm. "Come on, let's go someplace where we won't be spied on."

All of Tom's anger and frustration seemed to well up inside him like a coiled python. "Go ahead," he hollered at their retreating backs. "Next time, your *boyfriend* can come to your aid!"

Elizabeth spun on her heel. "That's right!" she shouted across the green. "But as long as you stay out of my way, that won't be an issue."

"You can count on that, Elizabeth," Tom muttered as she and Scott disappeared around the corner of the clubhouse. He looked down at his shaking hands. He didn't want to let Elizabeth walk away like this. But what choice did he have when seeing her with Sinclair tore his heart in two?

"Attention! Attention, please, all couples!" Lila's voice silenced the chattering groups having lunch on the patio. "I'm now putting up the schedule sheet for the mixed doubles tennis tournament. The first round matches will start in one hour. The second, third, and fourth rounds begin tomorrow at nine A.M."

Bruce looked up from his seat by the pool to the entrance of the clubhouse. Lila—now dressed in a short, white tennis dress that displayed her long, tan legs perfectly—was tacking a sheet of paper to the notice board. Within moments the space around the board was practically stampeded by a hoard of excited couples in tennis whites.

Weird, Bruce thought, watching everyone's reactions. He wanted to know who his and Lila's first opponents would be too, but these people were acting as if their lives depended on the tournament schedule. There was a lot of laughter, but even more shrieking, moaning, and groaning. One woman actually looked like she was close to tears as she fought her way through the crowd, away from the schedule.

Bruce got up and ambled over to where Lila had been squeezed against the wall. "What's with the locust plague?" he asked, gesturing to the bulletin board.

Lila shook her head, her full, red lips pressed tightly together.

"Frederick," Bruce heard a woman say in a harsh whisper, "we're paired with the Hawthorns." Her thick string of pearls wobbled as her breath came out in short gasps. "We're ruined."

"Impossible, Martha," Frederick stated sternly, looking around as if to be sure they weren't being overheard. "Get a grip on yourself. You must be reading it incorrectly. Everyone knows Trip Hawthorn has been taking lessons. It's impossible that anyone would want us to lose."

"I know that, you idiot," Martha whispered back sharply. "But it's right here on the schedule. Someone must have found out about the investigation into our finances!"

Bruce saw the man named Frederick elbow his wife aside to peer at the list. "Why, this is preposterous!" His eyebrows beetled into a ferocious frown which he turned on Lila. "Young lady, there's been a very serious mistake! Do you know who I am?"

Bruce watched Lila redden under the man's stare and instinctively put a protective arm around her trembling shoulders. "I'm sorry, Mr. Winslow," she said sadly, "but there hasn't been a mistake."

Mr. Winslow brandished his fist. "I demand an explanation!"

Bruce stepped between him and Lila. He'd been taught to respect his elders, and this man was a good thirty years his senior. But there was no way he was going to allow Lila to be threatened.

Mrs. Winslow rushed up to her husband, pulling at his jacket. "I'm sorry, Miss Fowler. We've been under a little strain lately. Come on, Frederick," she whispered.

Mr. Winslow's puffed up chest caved in and his shoulders drooped. He shook his head sadly and turned toward his wife. "How did they find out about the bank, Martha? How could we have sunk so low?"

Bruce gave Lila a questioning look as the couple despondently dragged themselves away. Even though they were obviously well-to-do, they seemed somehow out of place; perhaps it was because they were old enough to have their own children. *Grown* children. Older people were hard to come by at Verona Springs. Maybe the upper echelon of the club wanted to keep it that way. "What was all that about, Li?" Bruce asked, feeling uncomfortable.

Lila rolled her eyes. "It's a long story. Let's just say that if we play our cards right, we won't lose nearly as many games next year as we're going to lose this time."

Bruce cocked his head in confusion. He wasn't even going to begin to try to figure *that* one out. The crowd around the list had thinned and Bruce leaned in for a closer inspection. He traced his finger from his and Lila's name to . . .

"Awesome!" he hollered. "We're playing Bunny and Paul in the first round! In only one hour, we'll be mopping up the court with them!"

Lila's pretty features hastily drew into a scowl, dampening Bruce's excitement. "Shhh," she admonished, pulling him aside. "Don't count on it."

"What?" Bruce laughed. "This is a sure thing. I could play those two with my eyes closed. Paul can hardly walk across the floor without . . . *ooof!*"

Something as hard as a freight train had slammed into his body, sending him careening into the window of the clubhouse. He looked up, dazed, from where he lay in a flower bed, shocked that the window hadn't shattered and rained down on his battered body.

"Sorry there, chum," Paul gasped, untangling himself from Bruce and getting up. "This patio is, like, so uneven."

Bruce gingerly got up, brushing the dirt from his smarting palms on the sides of his tennis shorts. He gave Lila a meaningful look. "This is Paul Krandall."

Paul's hand shot up, knocking the tennis visor off her head. "Oh, sorry, *dear,*" he cried, dropping down to pick it up only to nearly topple over a table full of drinks. "Sorry, sorry."

Just then Bunny ran up. "Oooh, Bruce and Lila, I'm *so* excited we're going to be playing each other! Isn't it just *maaar*velous?"

"Yes," Lila replied graciously, "but if you'll excuse me, I have a few more arrangements to make."

Bruce started to follow her. He'd taken enough blows from Paul for one afternoon. But Bunny's long talons got a grip on his arm.

"Don't go yet, Bruce. You haven't told me how excited you are that we're playing together. After all," Bunny simpered, "we've got a real pro playing with us. Paul simply *loves* sports. He's a natural athlete. But don't worry, we'll try and keep Paul from beating you too badly. Won't we, Paul?" She turned to her fiancé. "You'll let poor little Bruce get in a shot or two, won't you, darling?"

"Sure," Paul agreed. "Teamwork's important. I'll make sure Bruce gets the ball plenty of times."

"Yes, sweetheart," Bunny smiled. "But remember, Bruce is on the *other* team. We want to get the ball *past* him."

"Huh?" But before Paul could comprehend that thought, he leaned against a potted fern, toppling himself and the plant onto the ground.

"Um, *yeah,* Bunny," Bruce agreed, masking his laugh with a cough. "I can see I should be *real* worried."

Bunny gave him a withering look before struggling with Paul's writhing body.

Bruce grinned. *Sweet revenge is a short tennis match away,* he thought gleefully. *Not only am I going to make Paul look like a fool, but I'm going to do it in front of the whole club! Bunny Sterling, eat your heart out! I'll show you how a* real *man plays tennis.*

"OK, Nick," Jessica mumbled. "I've passed whatever test of nerves you set up for me. Now where are you?" She shifted her weight from one leg to the other on the cracked sidewalk, trying to ease the pain in her toes. She'd shoved her feet into Isabella's too-tight, stiletto-heeled boots, and now they were starting to pinch. "I really *will* have to get a brand new wardrobe if I'm going to be expected to keep up *this* kind of vigil. Something, like, *orthopedic.* Who would have thought I'd be standing out on the street all day?"

She sighed and crossed her arms over her tight silver top. "No Nick, no anyone," she complained, glancing up and down the deserted sidewalk. "Except for that nerdy-looking guy across the street. All he needs is a yellow beanie to match his socks and he can try out for America's worst dressed man."

She rummaged through her bag and pulled out a small compact. All this waiting around under the bright afternoon sun was making her hot. She patted at her face with her powder puff. *Is that creep staring at me again?* she wondered. She turned around so that she could see his reflection in the compact mirror. Sure enough, he was squinting at her from behind his thick glasses. *What's his story?* He sticks out on that corner like a sore thumb. *And why does he keep peering over here? It's almost as if he knows me.*

Jessica gave a start. *He couldn't be that brainiac Rodney Putnick that I hung out with in high school for a week, could he?* Her face burned as she remembered the attempt she'd made—by pretending she was a nerd—to get Rodney to help her with her biology paper.

"No," she assured herself. "It couldn't be. What would Rodney be doing in a seedy neighborhood like this?"

But if it *wasn't* Rodney, why did the man keep staring at her?

Jessica snapped her compact shut and took a deep breath to steady her nerves. Regardless of who he was, she really wished he'd get lost. The last thing she needed was some egghead type stumbling into her undercover work. Nick would *surely* kick her off the case then.

And who knows, she thought, her palms turning sweaty, *maybe the bad guys are watching me right now—checking me out and trying to decide if I'm one of them or not.* "I may look the part," she murmured. "But if they see me talking to a geek, my cover will be totally blown!"

She shoved her compact back into her bag. She'd have to ignore the guy. Maybe he'd get the hint and go away. But when? And what if his mere presence was enough to ruin the whole operation? *I've got to get him to leave,* Jessica reasoned.

She sent the nerd across the street a nasty look. *I'm a tough, dangerous chick,* she told him telepathically. *So beat it!*

She smiled savagely as the Rodney look-alike jumped back, plastering himself against the brick wall. *That was easy,* she thought, tossing her long, black-streaked hair over her shoulder with a satisfied smirk. *If my career as an undercover cop doesn't work out, maybe I'll try my hand at being a clairvoyant.*

She closed her eyes and tried to put her newly found psychic powers to work. *"Om,"* she intoned. "You will now appear before me, Nick Fox." She opened her eyes. *Nothing.* Only the empty street and the geek on the other side.

Jessica unbuttoned the sleeves of her shirt and pushed them up to her elbow. This was getting ridiculous. Now she wasn't only hot, but seriously *annoyed* to boot. She fanned her face with her hand furiously. She'd never known Nick to be late. He'd better have a darned good excuse.

But what if Nick's decided not to work with me? she panicked. He hadn't exactly made a secret of his skepticism at her pleas to take her along on an investigation. "But Nick wouldn't just leave me here," she told herself. "Nothing would prevent him from coming, even if it was to tell me I was off the case. Nothing except . . ."

Suddenly Jessica didn't feel very well. Her eyes widened and her body tensed. Scenes of Nick in danger flashed through her mind. *He might have had an accident,* she thought suddenly. *Or worse—he could have been* made *by one of the criminals involved in this case!*

Jessica's lips drew together in a grimace as she remembered Nick's many close calls on his last job. Unbeknownst to Nick, Jessica had shown up at the chop-shop stakeout while he and his crew were making their arrests. She'd climbed up the fire escape and crawled out onto an overhead beam—giving herself a bird's-eye view of the scene below. The job had appeared to be going well. But they'd missed one man. He'd hidden during the raid and when no one was watching he'd popped up, holding a gun and pointed it directly at Nick.

Jessica had saved the day by flinging a hubcap at the gunman. *OK, so maybe it didn't come all that close to him,* she thought ruefully, *but at least it created a diversion.* She'd been able to scream a warning to Nick. The man had been apprehended and Jessica had rushed down from her perch. But then another man, one who even Jessica hadn't seen, appeared—this time holding a gun right against Nick's temple.

Jessica swallowed, reliving the terror she'd felt coursing through her body at the sight of Nick in danger. "But I came to his rescue," she murmured, smiling with relish at her bravery in bonking the crook over the head with a wrench. No one was going to mess with her boyfriend and get away with it.

See, Nick? she thought to herself. *We make a great team. You* need *me.* But was she too late now? She shivered, suddenly not warm at all, as if her blood had turned to ice. Had Nick run into some kind of trouble that, this time, she was helpless to avert?

"There's only one way to find out," Jessica murmured, trying to control the shakiness in her slender limbs. The nearest pay phone was on the corner across the street. Her apprehension at approaching the freaky geek was nothing compared to the terror she felt at the idea of something bad happening to Nick. "If the station house doesn't know what happened to him, then I'll have to assume the worst." She swallowed loudly as she stalked across the street with all the confidence she could muster. "Nick might be hurt . . . or already dead!"

*   *   *

Uh, oh, Nick thought, the adrenaline pumping through his veins. *Daryl's on the move. Should I tackle her now or tail her?* He gnawed at his bottom lip, torn between catching her off guard and hoping she might lead him right into her den of criminals.

He watched nervously as she continued to saunter confidently across the street. *But wait!* he thought. *She's stopping. She's reaching into her bag. She's pulling out something shiny. It's a . . .*

Nick streaked down the street a ways and dove behind a battered Oldsmobile, fully expecting Daryl to turn on him with a gun. His heart thudded like a big bass drum in his ears. He peered up above the car's dented hood. Instead of a gun, he could see the woman was simply holding a coin, which she inserted into the nearby pay phone.

She's making a call, he thought, relief flooding his body. *But to who? Joey the Tuna? Wall-eyed Eddy? Debster "Dead Shot" Johnston? Or one of her other nefarious associates?*

He had to stop her. Gun or no gun, Nancy Daryl was a menace to society. And it was Nick's job to make sure she was off the streets.

He ran commando-style from car to car until he was crouched against the back of the phone booth, his ear pressed to the metal wall, his breath coming hard and ragged. He could hear her long fingernails making sharp clicking noises as she punched in the numbers. He couldn't let that call get through. *Gotta make my move now,* he thought desperately.

Nick leapt out from behind the booth. "Reach for the sky," he hollered. "Nancy Daryl, you're coming with me!"

The woman whipped her head around; her mouth, lined with a garish, too-bright red lipstick, opened and closed like a stranded goldfish's before out popped one loud, terrified "Eeek!" She dropped the receiver and jumped back, throwing her arms in the air. Then she seemed to recover slightly. "Rodney? Is that you?"

Nick was just about to pounce and wrestle her to the ground when he stopped short. That voice was unmistakable—there was no other like it. It was the only voice that could send sweet shivers up and down his spine. "Jessica?" he croaked.

She lowered her dark glasses and stared at him, her aquamarine eyes as round as saucers. "Nick?" she gasped. "Where have you been? I mean, what are you doing? I mean . . . *who's Nancy Daryl?*" she shrieked jealously.

Nick crossed his brawny arms, the tight cuffs of his short-sleeved dress shirt cutting into his biceps. "Before you start giving me the second degree, who's *Rodney?*"

Jessica laughed. "I thought *you* were. Look at you—you look like a nerd!"

"And look at you!" Nick shot back. "I thought

you were a hardened criminal. Your hair's streaked black and . . . and you're wearing *vinyl pants!* You're dressed like a cheap slut!"

"Oh *no*!" they wailed in unison, the full impact of their mutual transformations hitting each of them like a ton of bricks. "*What* have you *done* to yourself?"

In a few more minutes Dana will be coming through that door, Tom thought glumly. *But that's not who I want to see.* He dropped down onto a bench outside the Verona Springs employees' lounge and hung his head.

"Get a grip, Watts," he scolded himself. "Elizabeth is with Scott now. He called her his girlfriend, and she said nothing to deny it. What more evidence do you need? An invitation to their wedding?"

Tom gripped the bench, the muscles under his light blue polo shirt bulging from the pressure. *But we were so close*, he thought, remembering the moment when she'd come to outside the greenhouse. *One more inch and I would have felt the softness of her lips again.*

"Forget about it," he growled. "As soon as Dana gets here, her kisses will help you forget all about Elizabeth. She's obviously wasting no time in forgetting about you."

Tom squeezed his eyes shut with a small grunt. The thought of Elizabeth entwined in Scott's arms was like a white-hot stab of jealousy piercing his heart. He forced the image away.

A low chatter from down the hall brought Tom to his senses. A few moments ago, the place had been empty. But now a steady stream of staff—waitresses, kitchen help, caddies—were heading for the lounge and pouring through the swinging double doors. *It must be break time,* Tom thought. *Or a changing of the guard.*

He sat up and nodded to a few of the employees who acknowledged him as they passed. For the first time, Tom noticed that all of the employees dressed in waitstaff uniforms appeared to be Latino. They traveled together in tight groups. Curiosity getting the better of him, Tom peered inside to see them take their places together, crowded around the rickety card tables that were set up in the room or on one of the two faded couches against the far wall. Most of the conversations were in Spanish. In fact, there was barely any English being spoken at all.

Tom tried to pick up a few words, but he'd been taking German since starting at SVU. His high-school Spanish was a dim memory now.

"Excuse me, amigo," a deep, only slightly accented voice intoned behind Tom, making him jump away from the door slightly. "Are you new here?"

Tom turned to see a stocky man in his twenties standing at his side. He was dressed in a white polo and crisp tan chinos—waitstaff garb—and his dark hair was styled perfectly. In his hand were a pair of sneakers and a duffel bag.

"I'm waiting for my girlfriend, Dana," Tom replied. "She's playing cello with the string quartet this afternoon."

"Ah, lovely," the man responded. "Music has always been one of my great joys."

"Mine too." Tom smiled.

The man held out his free hand. "My name is Carlos. Why don't you come inside and wait for your friend?"

Tom brightened. This could be a great opportunity to pick up some information—exactly what kind, he wasn't sure of yet. "Tom Watts," he introduced himself, shaking Carlos's hand warmly. "Thanks, Carlos. I appreciate it."

Tom followed Carlos inside and sat down on one of the folding chairs by the windows.

"Do you mind if I join you?" Carlos asked.

"Not at all."

Carlos sat and began to unlace his shiny black shoes. "My sister was a singer. In the old days, she had a voice that rivaled the songbirds."

"Doesn't she sing anymore?" Tom asked.

Carlos laughed. "She sings, only I no longer hear her. She's in Mexico."

"Have you been here long?"

Carlos pulled off his shoes, placed them in his duffel bag, and sighed. "Two years now."

"You must like it here," Tom commented, hoping to ease his way into some kind of revelation about the club.

Carlos shrugged and picked up one of his sneakers. "It's all right. I work very hard. Though sometimes I miss days of leisure and hearing my sister sing. In my village in Mexico, we could go months without anything exciting happening."

Tom nodded. "That sounds like the life. But I guess not that much happens at a country club either." Tom mentally crossed his fingers and hoped Carlos would take the bait.

"Mmm." Carlos cocked his head as if thinking. "That's true. Once in a while there's some confusion over one of the golf games or tennis matches, and voices will rise. But usually, things go smoothly."

Tom frowned. Could Carlos have been off the week of the murder? Even if he had, news of it must have run through the staff like wildfire. When Tom had worked as a caddy during high school, something as sensational as that—especially if it had happened to someone they worked with—would have been talked about for months, maybe even years. Tom scrunched up his face, pretending to think. "I seem to recall there being some sort of trouble here recently. Now . . . what was it?"

Carlos leaned over to tie his shoelace.

"Something about a caddy . . . ," Tom said.

Carlos kept his head bent.

" . . . and . . . someone drowning?"

Carlos looked up, his face blank. "I don't know. It's possible. The caddies and the waitstaff don't mix too much. They're mostly students from the university, you know. Too good to wait tables."

Tom scratched his jaw. "I guess you're right. Hmmm . . . maybe the police have already closed the case by now."

"Oh?" Carlos asked. "Do you think they might have?"

Tom spread his hands. "Don't know. I just remembered reading something about it. Maybe I was wrong." *And maybe the whole thing is being hushed up so nobody can talk about it,* Tom thought grimly. *Do you really know nothing? Or are you just too scared to talk?*

Chapter Six

"Ah, what a glorious day for a tennis match." Bruce laughed as he walked alongside Lila. He twirled his tennis racket expertly in his hand. "There's nothing like an afternoon trouncing to get the blood pumping."

He grinned and waved to a few people he knew. Already quite a crowd had gathered in the bleachers around the clay court where he and Lila would be playing Bunny and Paul.

Lila gave him a withering look as they walked onto the court. "You don't think we're going to *win* this, do you?" she whispered fiercely.

Bruce did a series of squats to stretch his hamstrings. "I've never been surer of anything in my life."

Lila dropped her tennis bag by a bench and pulled out a can of tennis balls. "Then be sure of this," she muttered. "We're *not* winning this game." She slipped a ball into the pocket of her tennis skirt.

Following Lila's lead, Bruce kept his voice low. "Don't be silly, Lila. Paul's a total klutz. It's the *second* round I'm worried about. This match is a given."

Lila narrowed her eyes and gave him a furious look. "A given that they *win.*"

"How can you think that?" Bruce murmured, pulling on his terrycloth wristband. "Even if by some miracle Paul didn't trip over his own two feet, you need *strategy* in this game, and between *these* two, they don't have enough brain power to light a thirty-watt bulb."

Lila brought her lips so close to Bruce's ear, he thought she was going to give him a good luck kiss. Instead came a blast of hot air. "Bruce, I'm *telling* you for the *last time,*" she threatened. *"Bunny and Paul win this match."*

"What?" Bruce gasped. He jumped up, practically knocking heads with her. "You mean you want us to *lose* to them on *purpose?* Throw the match?"

"Keep your voice down," she hissed, motioning furiously with her eyes toward the crowd surrounding them.

"Is there a problem?" the stern voice of the official called from his seat by the net.

"No, sir," Lila responded politely. "No problem at all." She lowered her voice again. "What do you think I've been saying? There'll be *no trouble*. OK, *sweetie*?" She spat out the term of endearment like it was a curse.

Just then Bunny and Paul appeared. Bruce watched, the juices in his stomach churning as their two opponents made their way toward the court. There were three wide slate steps leading down from the patio to navigate. Bruce held his breath, barely able to watch with one eye. Sure enough, Paul tripped over his feet and ended up landing in a flower bed.

Bruce cupped his mouth with his hand to keep in his laughter. "It would be impossible to lose to them," he spluttered. "Paul will be lucky to make it onto the court without a concussion." He turned to Lila, sure she'd understand.

Lila's cheeks were on fire. "I don't care if he spends every set flat on his back," she choked. "We *don't* win this match. *Capisce? They* do!"

Bruce shook his head. "No way." *If I let us lose this match to* them, he thought, *I'll look like an even bigger dimwit than Paul.* But before he and Lila could argue anymore, Paul and Bunny had spilled out onto the court. It was time to play.

"Not another point," Lila groaned. "Bruce is going to ruin us!"

Lila had been overwhelmed with satisfaction at how Bruce had toned down his game enough to allow Bunny and Paul to win the first set and then defeat them gently in the second—*for appearances' sake,* she had thought with relief. Going into the third and final set, it was an easy, unoffensive tie. All they had to do was sit back and let Bunny and Paul win the third, and they'd be home free.

Bruce had thankfully been lazy enough on the court to allow Bunny and Paul to advance two games. But in the twenty minutes since, she'd been watching helplessly as Bruce leapt and dove this way and that, gliding effortlessly across the court. Nothing seemed to get past him. Each ball he hit landed perfectly.

Bruce reared back and fired another powerful serve. A loud cry of derision came from the spectators as Paul once again swung wide and landed in a tangled mess, Bunny flattened beneath him.

"Game, Fowler and Patman," intoned the referee. "Four-two, Fowler and Patman."

Four games to two! If Lila and Bruce won two more games, they'd win the match. "This is social suicide!" Lila wailed.

Bruce turned and winked at her, flashing the thumbs-up sign. Lila scowled back at him. *He can taste victory,* she thought with exasperation. *But the only prize we're going to get is being kicked out of the club!*

She fought the tension in her shoulder as she waited for Paul and Bunny to get to their feet. *They really* are *the worst doubles team I've ever seen,* she thought. Bunny was a passable player. She at least could return the occasional ball. But Paul was *horrendous.* Worse than that, he was a *menace.* He'd already dropped his racket four times— once sending it flying into the bleachers!

Lila adjusted the sweatband around her forehead. "I've got to do something," she mumbled. "But what?"

I know, she thought. *I'll stop playing.* With Bunny serving, Lila let the next two balls pass by her without even lifting her racket. That gave Bunny and Paul a thirty-love lead. Two more points and they would have a game.

Bruce turned and gave her a dirty look. "This is *doubles,* Lila," he complained. "I'm not playing out here alone."

"Oh, yes you are, partner," Lila muttered. She let another ball get past her. *Forty-love.* One more point to go. She smiled at Bunny, encouraging her to hit toward her. But now Bruce got wise. Instead of leaving a section of the court open to Lila, he raced to the net on Bunny's serve, making the return before rushing backwards for the next volley.

Lila stamped her foot. "Get out of my way, Bruce!" she screamed.

He danced around her, lobbing back another ball. "Not until you start *playing,* my dear." He ran to the net and smashed a hard one down the middle of the court between Paul and Bunny. They collided again, but managed to stay on their feet. Bruce laughed, dancing backwards as Bunny again prepared to serve.

Lila narrowed her eyes. *I've been going about this all wrong,* she realized. *Maybe Bruce alone can mop up the court with Bunny and Paul, but he's going to have a much harder time if I actually* join *their team!*

This time when Bunny served, Lila jumped in front of Bruce and lobbed the ball into the bleachers. *Yes!* she thought.

"Game, Sterling and Krandall," cried the referee. "Four-three, Fowler and Patman."

Bruce growled. "Stay off my turf, Lila."

"Not a chance," Lila shot back. Now it was her turn to serve. Quickly she double faulted twice to make it love-thirty. *Can't make it too obvious, though,* she told herself. Elizabeth was probably in the audience, watching. They couldn't afford to arouse any suspicions.

She lobbed a nice easy serve directly to Bunny. When the ball came back over the net, she scooted around Bruce and deflected it off to one side, out of bounds. *Yes! Another point for Bunny and Paul!*

"I'm warning you!" Bruce fumed as she walked past him.

Lila smirked and served up another meatball. As Bunny's return came back over the net, she darted toward it, ready to intentionally misplay it again. But this time, Bruce was blocking her way.

No choice! she thought. She reared back and whacked him with her racket.

"Ow!" he cried, jumping sideways. The ball went sailing by.

"Game, Sterling and Krandall. Four-four tie."

"Yes!" Lila shouted. But unfortunately it was Paul's turn to serve. Lila groaned as he double faulted and then watched in agony as Bruce flawlessly powered the next serve back over the net, making it love-thirty in Bruce and Lila's favor.

"Stop it," Lila hissed.

Bruce tossed her a look that said *forget about it.*

Lila gritted her teeth and did her best to wrestle control of Paul's next serve away from him. But Bruce was on to her now, and his bigger bulk enabled him to keep her out of the action.

"Love-forty," said the referee. The game was almost over. If this kept up, Bruce and Lila would be within one game of winning the match!

The next serve from Paul and Bunny's side barely made it over the net. Lila immediately saw she wouldn't be able to reach the ball before Bruce did.

But I can reach Bruce, she thought, a new plan suddenly forming in her mind. As Bruce rushed forward, she kicked at his foot, knocking him off balance and causing him to land with a satisfying thud on the court.

"Ugh!" he cried.

"Fifteen-forty," the referee announced.

She leaned over and held out her hand. But instead of helping him up, she dug her long fingernails into his palm. "If you don't stop scoring points," she threatened hoarsely, "I'll put you in the hospital!"

"Fat chance," Bruce seethed. "Now that I know your latest trick, I won't let you near me."

Lila closed her eyes. If Bruce didn't listen to her, they were ruined. If they won the next point and then one more game, they would win the match—and be forever banished from high society.

She opened her eyes and looked at her boyfriend. "If they don't win," she hissed quietly, her voice as menacing as a snake's, "it's over between us."

Bruce swallowed loudly, the color draining from his face. "Lila, you can't mean that."

She nodded her head. "I've never meant anything more in my life."

Bruce closed his eyes in resignation. As much as it pained him, Lila could see that he had agreed. She helped him to his feet.

"May the best team lose," he whispered dejectedly.

Paul's next serve came over the net and Bruce did nothing to interfere as Lila hit the ball beyond the back of the court, into the crowd. *Thirty-forty.* Bruce returned the next serve by making a super-easy shot directly to Bunny, who hit the ball toward Lila. *Now I'll give Paul an easy one,* she thought to herself, tapping the ball lightly over the net. But Paul took two clumsy steps back, then changed his mind and tried to go forward again. *Disaster!* Paul's feet crossed and he went down like a brick.

"Game, Fowler and Patman!" the referee announced. "Five-four, Fowler and Patman."

Oh, no! No matter how badly Lila and Bruce played, Bunny and Paul were worse. "What are we going to do?" Lila cried. "One more game and we win the match!"

"Did you see that?" Scott gasped, clutching his sides. Lila had hit a tennis ball right into Bruce's back during the pivotal final game of their match. Elizabeth held out a steadying hand; Scott was laughing so hard, she was afraid he was going to take a tumble from their fourth row seats in the bleachers. "I hope all these socialites play this badly. If we don't get a story, maybe we'll get the trophy."

Elizabeth threw up her hands to cover her face as Paul's racket went flying through the air. "A bonk on the head is more like it," she groaned. "I've never seen such bad playing in my life. They make *me* look talented."

Scott turned to her and grinned. "If you're half as good at tennis as you are at everything else, I say we give up this investigative stuff and turn pro."

Elizabeth made a face. Scott's joking around might have been funny if their story was finished, or even if they'd made some progress on it. But since they hadn't, his attempts at humor only made her tense. "Scott, I don't mean to wreck your good time, but don't you think we should be off working on the story?"

"And miss checking out the competition?" he teased. "No way. But since you're not into winning the tournament, how about if we film these matches for the comedy channel? This stuff is priceless." He let out a loud guffaw as Paul nearly impaled himself on the net.

Elizabeth tossed her ponytail over her shoulder in an angry gesture. "I'm serious," she snapped. "I think we're wasting our time here."

Scott lurched forward, cupping his mouth with his hands. "Way to go, Lila!" He sat back and wiped a tear of laughter from his shining blue eyes. "Can you believe that? They're practically *tripping* each other now. They're funnier than the Marx Brothers!"

Elizabeth let out a low groan and crossed her arms over her white knit top. Now she was getting really annoyed. *Scott just doesn't get it,* she thought. *His investigative style is too casual. Tom would never waste valuable research time like this. Tom's* driven.

She took a deep breath as memories of Tom crowded her mind. If they were together now, they would be deep in discussion—bouncing ideas off of each other and plotting their next move. They were always in motion during an investigation. *Unless we were kissing passionately somewhere,* Elizabeth thought, a slight blush rising to her cheeks. *We did an awful lot of that too.*

Maybe I've been too hard on Tom, she pondered. *If I went to him, maybe we could team up for this story and at the very least put our journalistic differences aside—and maybe some other ones too.* She could almost feel his strong arms wrapped tightly around her, the slightly tangy scent of his aftershave making her dizzy with longing.

She took a quick glance around the bleachers, almost expecting to find Tom's handsome face smiling back at her. But she found only disappointment. The seats were crowded with club members showing off their latest tennis whites, golf garb, leisure slacks, and expensive designer sundresses.

He's out there investigating, Elizabeth thought. *He's not wasting his time watching this travesty.*

Suddenly Scott squeezed her hand and she jerked, startled by his touch.

"Relax, Liz. You're like a cat on a hot tin roof. We're soaking up atmosphere. It's important in a story to get the right *tone,* you know? Get to know the players in a piece."

Elizabeth rolled her eyes. "Scott, we already chatted with them, ate with them, and now we're watching them massacre a tennis game. I'm having a hard time thinking we're getting any closer. And with Tom out there . . . "

Scott looked at her, his blue eyes suddenly turning serious. "It's when they feel comfortable around you that they slip up." He ran a hand through his hair. "Don't worry about today. We got here too late to speak with the administrative staff anyway."

"But what about tomorrow?" Elizabeth cried. "If we just sit here, nothing will happen then either."

Scott gave her hand another squeeze. "All taken care of. While Tom was chasing you around the greenhouse, I made an appointment for you to interview the club manager. I gave the police station a try too. With a few more calls, it looks like I might be able to arrange a meeting with that Phillips guy."

"Really?" Elizabeth blurted excitedly. "That's great!"

"I *thought* you'd be pleased." Scott beamed. "So you can stop worrying. We're *way* ahead of Tom." He turned back to the tennis match and immediately started laughing as Paul and Bunny collided and began rolling around on the court, their tennis whites now almost completely clay red.

Elizabeth rested her elbows on her knees. *Maybe Scott's laid back style isn't so bad,* she realized. *In fact, Scott might turn out to be a better partner than I'd thought!*

"What's Elizabeth Wakefield doing here?" Dana grumbled. Suddenly the great mood she'd been in as she skipped through the beautiful gardens of the Verona Springs Country Club had come crashing down around her. Standing with the crowd at the far end of the main tennis court, Dana had caught a bright flash of all-too-familiar blond hair up in the bleachers—hair the color and silky texture of an angel's.

Dana clutched the metal railing that separated the standing spectators from the tennis court and drew in a long breath. From there she could just make out Elizabeth, seated in the bleachers, through a gap in the crowd. She was leaning forward, smiling, her gorgeous, serene face animated in conversation.

Dana craned her neck, dread filling her at the notion that it might be Tom that Elizabeth was talking to. *Don't look!* her mind screamed. *You don't want to know!*

She sprang back as if she'd been burned, narrowly missing a burly man carrying a bag of golf clubs. "What am I doing?" she cried. "It can't possibly be Tom up there with Elizabeth. Tom's waiting for me by the employees' lounge. In fact, he's probably worrying about where I am right now." She mentally kicked herself for having been seduced by the sound of the cheering crowd around the tennis court. But still she couldn't bring herself to leave.

That's right, Dana, a cruel voice taunted from inside her head. *Why go looking for Tom in the employees' lounge when he's obviously here?*

Dana plucked up her courage and again edged her way toward the railing, slipping around the burly man's arm. She leaned forward as far as she could, feeling the cold metal through her flimsy leopard print shirt. *No good.* At this angle she still couldn't make out Elizabeth's partner, and she was afraid her black leather mini-skirt was riding up a little too high. She would have to get closer—even at the risk of being seen by them.

"I can't," she blurted, tears flooding her large hazel eyes. The thought of coming face to face with Elizabeth and Tom together sent her heart racing.

She turned with the intention of slipping back through the crowd. But the circle of people surrounding her had gotten denser and now a solid block of bodies stood in her way. The only way she could leave was to walk right in front of the bleachers.

Please, don't see that I'm crying, Tom, she thought as she scooted under the railing and charged, head down, toward the exit. But as she turned to leave, her eye again caught the unmistakable flash of Elizabeth's blond hair and despite herself, she looked. In an instant, the cloak of pain and despair that had been shrouding her heart was lifted. It wasn't Tom at Elizabeth's side, but Scott Sinclair!

She hurried away from the tennis tournament, her heart swelling as she flew up the steps to the employees' lounge. It dropped a notch when she didn't see him sitting outside, but soared when she burst through the doors. "Tom!" she gasped as she came charging into the room. "You're here!"

Tom rose from where he was sitting with one of the waiters. "Of course. Are you all right?"

"Yes," she gushed, grabbing his hands. "I've never felt better." She felt like dancing and singing at the top of her lungs. *Tom is mine! Tom is mine! But even better,* she thought, *I'll make sure Elizabeth knows it too.* She tugged on Tom's hands, leading him toward the door. "Let's go for a walk. It's gorgeous outside."

"Sure," Tom agreed, looking at her sideways. "Whatever you say."

"Don't worry, I'm not crazy," she assured him, knowing exactly what was on his mind. *I'm just in love!*

"Finally," Bruce muttered resignedly as he deliberately let the winning tennis ball get past him. "It's over."

"Game, set, and match to Bunny Sterling and Paul Krandall," the official announced in a booming voice.

"Yeah!" Bunny screamed, jumping into Paul's arms. Paul spun her around in some sort of spastic celebration.

The crowd was roaring. *More with laughter than in admiration,* Bruce noted grimly, too embarrassed to even look into the bleachers. He wiped the sweat from his brow with his terrycloth wristband.

Lila came up to him and squeezed his arm. "You won't regret it," she whispered.

Bruce rolled his eyes. "I already do. I'm going to have nightmares about this for years," he grumbled.

"Come on," Lila murmured, urging him toward the net. "It's almost over."

Bruce froze. "You mean there's more?"

"We have to shake hands, silly, to show we're not sore losers." She pulled off her sweatband and ran her fingers through her satiny hair.

Bruce groaned. "I *am* a sore loser. My ego is in so much pain, it needs to be hospitalized."

Lila smirked and patted him on his broad, muscular back. "It wasn't that bad."

Bruce stared at her to see if she'd gone off her rocker. "*Not that bad?* That was the *worst* playing I've ever seen. *Bad* would have been if we'd been able to lose graciously. But Paul's so dismal, we had to twist ourselves up like pretzels just to let them win!"

"Hey Bruce," Paul called. He'd finally finished

his ludicrous victory dance and now had started running for the net.

"No, please!" Bruce gasped. But it was too late. He watched, paralyzed, as Paul—seemingly in slow motion—kicked out his gangly leg, leapt off the court a beat too late, and came crashing over the net. His body hit Bruce's like a Mack truck, the impact flattening Bruce against the ground.

This time there was no mistaking the laughter that exploded from the crowd. Bruce lay still, the wind knocked out of him for the umpteenth time that day. *Maybe if I stay here long enough,* he thought, *I'll wake up from this nightmare.*

Paul managed to dig both his heel and his elbow into Bruce's stomach before he climbed off of him.

"Come on," Lila whispered, gently tugging on his arm. "The coast is clear. You can get up now."

"No," Bruce insisted. "Let me sleep. I'll wake up in a second."

"Bruce, stop it. You still haven't shaken hands with Bunny."

Bruce shook his head back and forth vigorously. "Bad dream. Go away."

"What's the matter with Bruce?" Bunny sniggered. "Can't take losing? I *warned* you, Bruce, Paul's a devil with a tennis racket."

Bruce groaned. "Hang on," he told himself. "The alarm will go off in a few seconds."

Bunny tittered. "This is one dream you're *not* going to wake up from! We're the champs! We're the champs!"

"That's it," Bruce growled, snapping his eyes open. He leapt to his feet. "Your playing *stunk!*"

"Sore loser!" Bunny taunted, swatting him with her racket.

"I'll sore loser *you,*" Bruce hollered, lunging for her.

Bunny squealed and ran behind Paul.

"Stop it!" Lila screamed. She jumped in front of Bruce, her brown eyes flashing furiously. "Remember what I said."

"No," Bruce groaned, clutching his head. "You can't break up with me over this."

"Oh yes I can," Lila hissed. "Now shake Bunny's hand."

"Ha-haaa!" Bunny bounced toward him and reached out her bony claws.

Bruce took a deep breath and leaned toward her. She grasped his hand. But instead of shaking, she yanked with all her might, knocking him off balance. Bruce found himself sprawled out on the court yet again, his face flaming red, and the crowd in the bleachers in utter hysterics.

Chapter Seven

I guess I was wrong, Elizabeth thought bitterly. *Tom wasn't off investigating the murder story. He was with Dana!* She felt her sea-green eyes begin to sting as she watched Dana nestle herself against him as they settled into the bleachers across the court.

"I can't believe I actually started to care about him again," she whispered under her breath. "What will it take to get it through my thick head? Tom and I are finished!"

"What's that?" Scott asked, turning to her. "Do you have a headache?"

"No, well . . . maybe a little," Elizabeth mumbled, looking down at her hands. "I think this sun is getting to me." *Heartache is more like it,* she thought. But she couldn't very well tell Scott that. As far as he knew—or anyone, for that matter—she was long over Tom. *But why don't I know that?*

Scott hopped up. "We'll go, then. The next first-round match doesn't start for fifteen minutes."

Elizabeth had just stood up to follow him when her eyes locked with Dana's. Her heart gave a lurch. There was a tight smile on Dana's full lips and, even from across the tennis court, Elizabeth could see a malicious gleam in her big, hazel eyes.

Dana tossed back her dark, curly hair and put a proprietary hand on Tom's cheek. She lifted his sunglasses and then drew him close to her for a long kiss.

Elizabeth's face crumpled and she sat down hard on the bench.

"Liz, are you OK?" Scott asked, his face full of concern.

"Yes, I'm fine," she managed to squeak, her uneven voice coming back to her through the thudding, racing blood in her ears. She pressed trembling fingers to her forehead.

"Are you sure? You look like you saw a ghost."

Elizabeth nodded, swallowing back a sob.

"We'd better go," Scott insisted. "Sunstroke can get pretty rough."

Elizabeth shook her head, breathing deeply over the tears that were crowding her throat. "No . . . let's stay until the crowd thins." There was no way she was going to let Dana think she'd run her off.

Scott spread his hands in a gesture of surrender. "Whatever you want."

"I'll be ready in a moment," Elizabeth explained. She had one more thing to do. She took a deep breath to steel herself. She'd known this would happen sooner or later. And now that it had, she would prove she could survive it.

She held her head high and looked back at Tom and his new girlfriend. Their kiss had ended and Tom's sunglasses were covering his eyes again. Tom started suddenly when he looked in Elizabeth's direction and she knew he'd just noticed her—though it was hard to read what he felt.

But I'm sure I can guess, Elizabeth thought. She squared her shoulders and set her face in a determined smile. *Since you obviously don't care about me anymore, then I hope you can see I don't care about you either. And I'll do whatever it takes to keep you from thinking otherwise!*

"Calm down, Watts," Tom told himself. His heart was booming in his chest like a string of firecrackers. He hadn't expected to see Elizabeth. He gripped the seat of the bleacher, thankful he was sitting for the dizziness hitting his brain. And even more thankful that he was wearing his dark sunglasses so that the longing in his eyes didn't betray him.

"Was that kiss too much for you?" a soft voice teased. Dana's low, sultry tone broke into his thoughts, reminding him he wasn't alone. He blinked, looking blankly at the woman who moments before had thrilled and enticed him as she burst into the employees' lounge calling his name. Her leopard print shirt and tight leather miniskirt showed off her curvy figure to perfection. Some days she dressed like an animated rag doll, others like she was a debutante readying herself for combat. But today he couldn't help but swell up with pride as all heads had turned to admire her cool, sexy look.

"You're breathing awfully heavily," Dana continued. She glanced at him through her long, full lashes and finally everything fell back into place.

"No, I'm fine, Dana," Tom replied, trying to keep the coolness out of his voice. She was talking about their kiss, which he'd enjoyed until he'd realized Elizabeth had witnessed it. Then he'd felt as if his lips had become parched, leaving a dry, bitter taste in his mouth.

"Good," Dana gushed, running a hand through her glossy mahogany hair. Her laughter, usually so bright and chime-like, sounded brittle to his ears. "Because there's more where that came from." She reached for him, wrapping both arms tightly around his neck.

But this time Tom pulled back. Instead of feeling the warm desire of her embrace, it felt as if octopus tentacles were trying to enslave him. He'd wanted to hurt Elizabeth before, when he'd called

Dana with her standing right there and sweet-talked her so blatantly. In fact, he'd *enjoyed* it. Why was he resisting her now?

He winced when he saw the pained confusion on Dana's beautiful face. He didn't mean to hurt her. But with Elizabeth around, all his affection for Dana seemed to fly from his heart.

"What's the matter?" Dana asked, her soft lips pouting.

"Nothing," Tom replied.

"Yes there is," Dana insisted. "One minute you like me and the next . . . you push me away."

Tom shook his head. "Just give me a minute."

"Why?" Dana asked, her bottom lip trembling.

Because, he responded silently, *I'm trying to remember why I liked you in the first place!* "Please, Dana, I need a little air."

Tom thrust his hands into the pockets of his chinos. At any other time, Dana would have been perfect. She was smart, classy, and a passionately talented musician. Her only flaw was that she wasn't Elizabeth.

Tom swallowed hard as he looked at Dana's steely profile. She'd drawn away from him and was staring morosely across the tennis court. Guilt crept into him. He hated leading her on, but he needed her in order to pursue his story. *Time might change my heart,* he thought. I could come to love her. And if anyone could help exorcise his feelings for Elizabeth, it was Dana.

"Maybe your kisses *were* too much," he joked, trying to coax a smile back onto her lips. He took her hand and patted it—a gesture that Elizabeth wouldn't be able to see.

Dana pulled her hand away and started to toy with the hem of her black leather mini. "I'd like to think that, but I noticed Elizabeth was across the way."

Tom could feel himself redden under Dana's stare. "She has nothing to do with this," he stated flatly. In a softer tone he added, "I just have a lot on my mind."

"OK . . . as long as that's all it is."

Tom nodded and, despite himself, shot a look over to where Elizabeth was sitting. For a moment he was mesmerized as he watched her slender figure, in a long blue skirt and white top, descend the stairs. Then suddenly a large woman, obviously in a hurry, banged into her.

Tom felt his breath catch as Elizabeth started to stumble and pitch forward. His heart leapt to his throat, her name on the tip of his tongue. But in that split second, Scott reached out and grabbed her around the waist, pulling her into his arms. As she tilted her head up to thank him—lips parted, a bright smile lighting up her face—Tom was told everything he needed to know.

He dropped his eyes and swallowed bitterly. "I'm ready now, Dana," he growled, taking Dana roughly in his arms and turning all the hurt he felt into the passion of his kisses.

* * *

"I can't believe you, Jess," Nick complained. He dumped two sugar cubes into his coffee and gave the dark brew a brisk stir. "We're supposed to be infiltrating a country club, not a biker bar."

Jessica leaned back in the squeaky, torn vinyl booth in the run-down diner and groaned. "How was I supposed to know that?" she protested. "All your other assignments are down and dirty."

He took off his thick glasses and massaged his temples. "Exactly. That's why I didn't want you to go on any of them with me. But this case wouldn't be a stretch for you. With your *former* blond good looks, you could have easily passed for a country club type—and been a perfect cover for me."

Jessica toyed with one of her temporarily black strands. "Thanks a lot. It's *not* like this stuff is permanent or anything. And anyway, it sounds to me like *I'll* be playing the decoy while *you're* the one having all the fun."

Nick smirked and started to run a hand through his hair. "Yuck," he groaned, staring at his fingers. The greasy stuff he'd used to plaster it back was thick on his fingers.

Jessica giggled. "The wet head is dead."

Nick made a face. "Very funny. But let's get back to you. There's no way they're going to let us into the Verona Springs Country Club with you looking like an escapee from cell block *H*."

Jessica winced. Verona Springs! *Of all the country*

clubs in the world, she thought, please *don't let it be that one.* "Um . . . *which* club did you say?"

"Verona Springs," Nick repeated. "A caddy was murdered there, and another caddy is being held on suspicion. But I think we've got the wrong guy. A call came in last night from some nervous old man with a Spanish accent telling us that the real killer is still on the loose. Do you know the country club?"

Jessica nibbled on her bottom lip worriedly. "More like it knows me. Or at least a couple of the members do."

Nick folded the paper and placed it back in his pocket. "That's OK. That'll make our cover look even more natural. You're a regular. We have a built-in excuse to be there."

Jessica blanched. "Nick . . . um, I have a confession to make. There's a slight, teensy-weensy, itty-bitty little problem."

Nick reached for his coffee and took a gulp. "Oh? What's that?"

"Well, um . . . Lila goes to that club. She's my best friend, Nick."

Nick shrugged. "All the better. She can introduce us around. That'll make our work a lot easier."

"No, you don't understand. I, um . . . how do I say this . . . " Jessica flipped her hair behind her shoulder and, as quickly as she could, blurted it out. "I told her that you were taking me along on your next assignment. OK?"

"What!" Nick hollered. His cup came crashing down, sloshing coffee onto the Formica table. "*Jessica!* What did I *tell* you was the *first* rule of undercover work?"

Jessica covered her face with her hands. "Make sure to have exact change in case you need to make a phone call?"

"Jessica!"

She giggled nervously and peeked out from between her fingers. "Make sure you water your plants, because it might be a while before you come back home?"

Nick gave her a stern look. "I'm warning you."

Jessica sighed and dropped her hands. "OK, OK, I give in. *Don't tell people when you're going undercover.*"

"Exactly." He ran his napkin over the coffee puddle. "I'm going to have to get someone else."

"No!" Jessica cried. "Oh, Nick, that's not *fair!* I'm *perfect* for this assignment."

Nick shrugged his broad shoulders once again. "That's right. But what else can I do? The minute Lila sees us at the country club, our cover's blown."

She grabbed his arm. "Wait. I'll come up with something." She narrowed her blue-green eyes, her mind working overtime. *I've got it!* she thought. "Nick, look at me!"

He flicked his eyes in her direction. "Yeah?"

"What do you see?"

Nick laughed. "I already told you. A sleazy biker chick."

Jessica tapped the table. "Exactly. And you *didn't* recognize me, did you?"

Nick folded his muscular arms across his chest. "I also told you that Verona Springs would never let a biker chick onto the premises."

Jessica waved his comment away. "But they would let in someone *else*—someone *different*. Someone with extreme beauty and wealth, with a touch of the exotic."

"But Lila knows you—," Nick started.

Jessica held up her finger to silence him. "If you ever got a good look at my makeup drawer, you would *know* I'm the woman of a thousand faces."

Nick slowly smiled at her as understanding dawned on his chiseled features. "You *did* do a great job of disguising yourself."

Jessica sat back with smirk. "That's right."

"Are you thinking what I'm thinking?" they cried in unison.

"Everything's going great, don't you think?" Lila asked brightly. "Look at my master list. I'm going to have to start turning people away." She held up the piece of paper for Bruce's inspection.

Bruce only grunted and stared off across the patio, his blue eyes lost in thought.

Lila sighed and tossed the sheet on the table between them. *He'll get over it sooner or later,* she thought. *Especially when we're welcomed into the land of exclusive VIP-dom.* "I know you hate losing, Bruce, but look what it's doing to our social life."

Bruce grabbed his iced tea and took a swig. "Some social life," he grumbled. "I'm the laughingstock of the whole place." He put his elbows on the table and rested his chin despondently between his hands.

Lila pushed back her silky hair and adjusted the collar of her tennis top. "That's not true. And anyway, what do *you* care about a stupid little tennis game?"

Bruce narrowed his eyes. "Nothing if I win it. But . . . "

"Oh look, there's Pepper." Lila waved gaily. She turned back to Bruce and lowered her voice. "You'll see how things have changed already."

"Yeah, right."

"Oh, Pepper," Lila called brightly. "Hi, Pep!"

Pepper started slinking their way. Her pink and green one-piece bathing suit looked as if it were cut for a granny, but Lila regarded it with jealousy anyway. *I wonder where she picked* that *gorgeous little thing up?* she wondered.

"Going for a swim?" Lila asked.

Pepper dropped down on the empty seat at their table. "Not now, when I can sit and sip tea with the new belle of the ball."

Lila tittered. She could almost hear an invitation to join the VIP Circle behind Pepper's words.

"The match *did* go smashingly well, didn't it?"

Pepper winked. "Couldn't have gone better."

"Oh, *please,*" Bruce blurted. "I could think of a *number* of ways—"

Lila kicked him hard under the table. "Why don't you go get Pepper an iced tea, *darling.*"

Rubbing his shin, Bruce glared at her. "In a minute. I was just saying—"

Lila gave him her harshest warning look. They hadn't gotten this far for Bruce to blow everything on account of his bruised ego! "Bruce, I'm *not* sure you *understood* me. Pepper's thirsty *now.*"

Bruce met her eyes, his own blazing. But Lila knew he was an amateur when it came to waging a staring war against her. Finally he backed down, and Lila let out a small sigh of relief. "Thank you, *sweetie.* Pepper prefers her iced tea with lime."

Bruce pushed back his chair roughly. "Then lime it is."

Lila watched until he was safely at the terrace bar before turning back to Pepper. "Boys. They *hate* to lose."

Pepper laughed. "But you did it so *well.* Bunny and Paul *couldn't* be happier."

Lila smiled. "We were just happy to get the opportunity to play them."

"That's good." Pepper reached over and picked an invisible piece of lint off Lila's tennis top. "And you played the game beautifully, if you know what I mean."

Lila's eyes sparkled as she reveled in the part of the conversation that remained unspoken. *Almost there,* she thought. *Pepper's bound to ask us to join the VIP Circle any second!* "You know, Bruce and I *like* to be accommodating. It's in our nature."

Pepper flicked back a strand of her white-blond hair. "I can see that. I can also see that you fit in this club *very* well—the way you present yourselves, etcetera, etcetera . . . .I'm *sure* if you continue to—shall we say—*act* like one of us, you two will have a *wonderful* future here."

Lila beamed. *VIP Circle, here we come!*

"An iced tea with lime," Bruce ordered. He took a seat at the terrace bar and leaned his elbows grumpily on the polished wood. *I can't deal with Lila anymore,* he thought bleakly. *She couldn't care less that I came out looking like a total loser on the tennis court today. To the contrary, she was completely thrilled!*

"An iced tea with lime," the slim bartender repeated. "Yes, sir. Can I get you anything else?"

"A new life?" Bruce quipped. *One with a thriving ego,* he added silently.

The bartender nodded and bit his lip. Bruce got the strangest feeling that the man was taking him seriously.

"I wish I could help you, sir," the bartender responded, his face was turning a dusky brick color, almost as if he were choking.

"Are you all right?" Bruce asked, jumping up. If the man was really suffocating, he'd give him the Heimlich maneuver and save his life.

The bartender jumped back and then a look of sheer panic crossed his face. He threw himself forward, wrapping his arms protectively around the glassware on the counter. "Please sit down, sir. I'm fine." A giggle escaped from his mouth.

Bruce sat down hard and peered at him. "You weren't choking at all. Were you?"

"No sir." The bartender grinned, more laughter seeping out from the sides of his mouth. He straightened up and dabbed at his dark brown eyes with a cocktail napkin. "I'm fine. I'll make your drink now."

What, is the help *laughing at me too?* Bruce wondered, reaching down the bar to grab a handful of nuts from a small glass bowl. Instantly another bartender—this one chunky with dark, wavy hair—dove across from his section and slid the bowl in front of Bruce. "Here, sir, don't strain yourself."

Bruce scowled. The chunky bartender's inky-black eyes were dancing with laughter as well. When the slim bartender came back with a cool-looking drink in a tall frosted glass, Bruce reached out to take it from him. But the man smoothly pulled his hand back. "I'll carry that for you, sir."

What?" Bruce asked. "I'm just taking it to that table over there." He pointed across the patio to where Lila and Pepper were locked in animated conversation.

"I know, sir," the bartender replied. "But we always carry Mr. Krandall's drinks."

Bruce frowned. "I've never seen you carry anybody else's." *Boy,* he thought. *I hadn't realized Paul was such an important VIP that the barstaff waits on him hand and foot.*

"I'm sorry, sir," the slim bartender squeaked. "But it's club policy."

"Since when?" Bruce demanded. "I carried my own drinks this morning."

The slim bartender spluttered. "Glass breaks easily when you drop it."

Bruce felt his head spinning. "What's that got to do with me?"

Both bartenders took a step back, their faces incredulous.

Bruce narrowed his eyes, shocked awareness suddenly dawning on him. "OK, that's *it!*" he hollered, slamming his fist on the counter and sending both bartenders to the ground, covering their heads. "You guys think I'm a klutz, don't you?"

The bartenders looked up and, realizing nothing had come crashing down around them, slowly stood. The slim bartender sheepishly brushed dust from his pants. "We heard about your tennis match with Mr. Krandall, sir."

The chunky, wavy-haired one nodded vigorously. "Anyone who could lose to him . . . well . . ."

Bruce's mouth dropped down to his chest. "Give me that drink," he scowled. He grabbed the iced tea and turned to storm off across the patio. His face was beet red and his hands were shaking with fury. *This is all Lila's fault,* he thought. *She made me lose that stupid game! Well, from now on, this charade is off. I'm going to show everyone I'm . . .*

But suddenly he felt himself flying through the air. Before he knew it, Bruce found himself face down, sprawled across the flagstones, the glass of iced tea smashed to smithereens and a barstool on top of him. The untied lace of one of his sneakers had somehow looped itself around the bottom rung of the barstool.

As everyone on the patio erupted into laughter, the few tattered remains of Bruce's ego were flattened into dry, tasteless pancakes. "And I bet Lila couldn't be happier," Bruce muttered.

Chapter Eight

"I'm sure we're on the right track," Elizabeth murmured as she and Scott started down the lighted path that wound through the SVU campus.

"I hope so," Scott teased. "I'd hate to think we got lost walking from the parking lot to your dorm room. But your head has been in the clouds since we parked your Jeep, so I guess anything is possible."

Elizabeth smirked. "I meant the right track for our *story,* not our hike to Dickenson Hall."

Scott laughed. "I know. I just wanted to see if *you* knew. Especially since you seem to have forgotten I'm here."

Elizabeth gave him a sideways glance. Scott was certainly astute. "Sorry . . . I was thinking about what I'm going to say tomorrow when I interview the club manager."

As they passed the bright lights of the campus

coffee house, Elizabeth noticed there were still a few couples deep in conversation, their eyes filled with love and longing. *Tom and I used to be like that,* she thought. *Back when he still loved me.* She tore her gaze away, feeling suddenly heartsick at the memory. She sped up and stepped over the small hedge bordering the track, taking the short-cut across the running field. In the distance the few remaining lights of the library winked at her. *Tom has a new love now,* they seemed to say.

Elizabeth shivered and pulled her blue gabardine jacket tighter across her chest. The cool evening breeze had shifted and she could hear the sounds of music from Fraternity Row carried along with it. *Maybe Tom's dancing with Dana at one of those parties,* she thought.

"Elizabeth, slow down!" Scott begged.

She looked up and realized he was panting. Even though he'd been walking close at her side, she'd felt as if she was the only single person out that night—alone and unloved.

He took a deep breath. "In answer to your question, I think since we told Lila that we're writing a story on the mixed doubles tennis tournament, it's probably best to stick with that cover."

"Hmmm," Elizabeth murmured, again lost in thought. She'd noticed a light on in the WSVU building across the way. *No, Tom's probably working away there, at WSVU, right now. Is Dana with him?* She flinched and turned her attention back to Scott. "I guess you're right. But that makes it harder to slip in questions about the drowning."

Scott sucked in his bottom lip. "That's true. But maybe the club manager will bring it up himself. Or you could mention it, and if he balks, assure him anything he says is off the record. After all, you're writing a society piece."

Elizabeth's eyes suddenly glowed. All her gloomy thoughts about Tom and Dana were pushed away as her enthusiasm about tomorrow's interview began to rise. "Yes! And if he refuses to talk about the drowning, that'll show he has something to hide."

Scott gazed at her with open admiration. "Another star for the ace reporter!"

Elizabeth laughed. "Make that for two ace reporters. I couldn't have gotten there without you."

Scott blushed and his smile widened. "I'm just a sounding board."

"That's not true at all," Elizabeth insisted. "I couldn't do this story without you."

"Really?" Scott asked.

Elizabeth turned to him with a big smile. "Really. You've been a great help."

They'd reached the stone steps outside Dickenson Hall, the modern glass-faced dorm where Elizabeth lived with her twin sister. As she opened the door, she turned to say good-bye to

Scott, but he pushed himself in behind her.

"Um . . . I'm home," she said lamely, throwing him a questioning look.

He smiled. "So you are."

Elizabeth let out a nervous little laugh. "I can find my way upstairs now."

"I'm sure you can."

Elizabeth frowned and started toward the staircase—alone. Memories of last evening—when Scott grabbed her in the Jeep, his lips pressing against hers forcefully, unbiddingly, not stopping even after she'd said no—filled her mind and she suddenly didn't feel so comfortable anymore. She trotted briskly for the stairs, pausing at the bottom to make sure that Scott had left her alone for the night.

The pause was a mistake. Within seconds Scott was next to her, and then he was practically on top of her. She looked up, startled to find his lips so close to hers that she could feel his warm breath caressing her face. She tried to step away, but she was trapped, pinned against the wall.

"Was that Dana on the phone?" Danny asked.

Tom leaned back in his desk chair and looked over at his roommate. Danny was already lying in his single bed, his muscular arms propping up his head, a copy of Walt Whitman's *Leaves of Grass* open on his bare chest.

"None other than," Tom said tiredly. "She

wants me to go to the Verona Springs Country Club again tomorrow."

Danny sat up, the book tumbling off him onto his green muslin bedspread. "That's good, right?"

Tom pulled off his sneaker and let it drop to the floor. "I guess."

Danny frowned. "But you like her, don't you? I mean, you'd have to be blind not to notice how gorgeous she is."

Tom sighed and pulled off his other sneaker, shoving them both under his bed. "Yeah, I like her."

Danny grabbed an extra pillow from the floor next to his bed and punched it before putting it behind his head. "You don't sound very excited. Maybe you don't like redheads."

Tom groaned, pulled off his polo shirt, and tossed it into the open clothes hamper. "I like redheads fine. But Dana's hair is more mahogany. . . . What do you care, anyway?"

"So you noticed."

Tom stood up, pulled off his chinos, and draped them over his desk chair. "What's that supposed to mean?"

"Her hair color. You actually care enough to know what it is."

Tom scowled. "I have no clue what you're getting at, Danny."

Danny cocked his head slightly to the side and studied him. "When you were talking to Dana before, you sounded as if you were all in love and everything. I glanced over, expecting you to have that goofy I'm-on-top-of-the-world look. But I could have sworn that you had been discussing *funeral arrangements* instead of a date. It was kind of freaky."

Tom turned away and busied himself by setting his alarm clock. "I'm just tired. Remember, I was up all last night in the research room."

Danny grunted. "You've pulled all-nighters before. But anytime Elizabeth called, even if you'd been dead on your feet a second before, you'd be up and ready for anything."

Tom plucked his striped pajama bottoms from under his pillow and pulled them on before slipping between the coolness of his fresh blue sheets. All he wanted right now was to hit the sack. "That was because Elizabeth was my reporting partner," he explained wearily. "We fueled each other's excitement."

"Hmmm," Danny murmured as if he were clearly unconvinced. "Then if that's all it was, then maybe you should ask Liz to be your partner again."

Tom yanked the covers up to his chin. "She already has a boyfriend. Scott Sinclair."

Danny turned off the light by his bed. "I meant partner as in *reporting partner,* not *girlfriend*. But now that you mention it, maybe asking her out wouldn't be a bad idea either."

Tom squeezed his fists. "Have you forgotten the letter I wrote her?" he asked sourly. It had been at Danny's prompting that he'd written his declaration of love for Elizabeth in the first place—and that had done nothing but leave him feeling raw and exposed as Elizabeth ignored him and flaunted her new boyfriend around in front of him. "She hasn't exactly responded to it, you know. Unless you call throwing herself at Scott Sinclair a positive sign."

Danny sighed. "Liz might need time to realize that you're not mad at her anymore. You hurt her pretty badly."

Tom snapped off his light. Already he could feel an uncomfortable burning behind his eyes, and there was no way he wanted Danny to catch him feeling emotional. "Don't remind me," he snarled, furtively wiping a tear with the back of his hand.

Even when Tom hadn't believed Elizabeth's story about his biological father's behavior, he'd felt tortured about breaking up with her. Now that he knew she'd been telling the truth, his angry words and callousness toward her were like a constant pain in his heart.

"What I mean is," Danny began, "maybe she needs you to approach her again. In person. Not by letter. Really show her how you feel."

Tom flopped over onto his stomach. "I don't think it matters how I feel anymore," he mumbled into his pillow. "What matters is how *she* feels. And right now her feelings seem to be for Sinclair."

For a while Danny was silent. All Tom could hear was the faint whirring of his alarm clock. He closed his eyes, thinking Danny had fallen asleep. He felt himself begin to doze. But then his friend's low voice crept through the darkness. "Then maybe it's time to move on."

Tom rolled onto his back, one arm flung across his face. "To where?" he asked sleepily.

Danny's voice seemed to come from far off. "Dana," he suggested. "Instead of just *pretending* you like her, why don't you start *really* liking her?"

Tom took a deep breath, fighting to stay awake a little longer. "I've *tried*. That's easier said than done."

"Maybe," Danny said levelly. "But I bet if you stopped fighting her, it would be a lot easier than you think. Unless I'm missing something, Dana really likes you."

Tom felt himself drifting back into sleep. "Dana . . ." he managed. Her feelings for him were straightforward and uncomplicated. *At least she likes me,* he thought, *unlike* . . .

But before Tom could complete the sentence, he was enveloped in soft, dark slumber.

"Scott, no," Elizabeth protested. With her back to the wall and Scott directly in front of her, she had nowhere to turn. She looked up as Scott's face loomed even closer. His eyes were closed, but his lips were on autopilot. *And there's no doubt about where he thinks they're landing,* she thought desperately. She raised her arms, ready to fend him off if necessary. Then, just as it seemed Scott's lips couldn't get any closer, she noticed a space under his right arm large enough for her to duck under. She slipped out from his grasp and burst up the stairs, hearing him stumble as his lips more than likely met plaster and paint.

"I'll see you tomorrow," she chirped, pushing her way through the second-floor fire door and hearing it lock behind her. She breathed a sigh of relief. "Scott just can't take a hint," she groaned as she walked to her room and fumbled with her keys. "*Now* what am I supposed to do?"

But before she could answer her own question, the door to the room flew open. "Jessica!" Elizabeth exclaimed. "What are you doing?"

Jessica was attempting to back out of the room, dragging a huge, obviously heavy suitcase with her. She jumped and whirled around in one motion. "Liz!" she cried, blushing crimson. "I, um, I left you a note."

Elizabeth raised a questioning eyebrow. "That suitcase is large enough to hold both your wardrobe *and* mine, Jess. Are you taking off with my clothes?"

Jessica snorted and adjusted the oversized beret

on her head. All her golden-blond hair had been stuffed underneath it, giving her head a preposterous, muffin-top look. "I don't think I'd ever be that desperate."

"Very funny," Elizabeth replied. Even though she and Jessica were identical twins—with the same delicate features, blue-green eyes and slim, athletic bodies—sometimes their appearances were *all* they had in common. Especially when it came to fashion sense. Jessica went for clothes that created a stir. Slim, sexy, skin-baring, shimmery, shiny—if her clothes didn't make her the center of attention, then something was horribly wrong.

Elizabeth took a quieter, more measured approach—jeans and T-shirts were fine by her. She found there were enough explosions in life without having to be the one to set them off. *Though lately it seems like I'm at ground zero no matter* what *I wear,* she thought miserably.

Elizabeth narrowed her eyes at her sister. "Speaking of clothing—why are you wearing that beret? Did you do something to your hair?" She reached out a hand toward her sister's head.

"Stop!" Jessica cried, pushing Elizabeth's arm away. "It was just a little . . . fashion faux pas," she explained, regaining her composure. "Now let me out before I'm late. Isabella's waiting for me downstairs in her car."

Elizabeth shook her head. "Not until you tell me where you're going, Jess." She had enough on her plate right now without having to worry about her twin. Jessica's taste in clothing wasn't the only wild thing about her. She had a habit of finding hot water no matter where she went. And all too often Elizabeth ended up having to be the one to bail her out—sometimes literally. Maybe this time she could stop whatever trouble Jessica was getting into before it started.

Jessica groaned, clasping and unclasping her hands.

"C'mon, Jess, I'm not getting out of your way until you tell me where you're going."

Jessica gulped audibly, but then her blue-green eyes turned innocent. "Isabella and I are taking some Theta rushes on a road trip."

Elizabeth's brow knitted skeptically. Since when was Jessica reluctant to talk about a sorority outing? *Wait a minute!* she thought. *Why should I stand in her way? If Jessica's going out of town,* now *would be the perfect time!* Even though Jessica had a knack for getting into trouble, Elizabeth had to admit that her own journalistic exposés had landed them both in the soup on more than a few occasions. *At least* this *time, if anything goes haywire,* she thought, I'll *be the only one who gets burned!*

Smiling, Elizabeth stepped aside and held the door open so that Jessica could easily pass through. "Bon voyage, Jess."

Jessica gave her a suspicious look, but didn't

say anything as she waddled through the door with the enormous suitcase.

"I really mean it," Elizabeth insisted. "Have a nice trip. Tell Izzy I said hi." She helped push the suitcase the last few inches out the door and, after slamming the door shut, heaved a humongous sigh of relief. "This is perfect," she whispered. The more she thought about it, the more obvious it seemed—having Jessica underfoot was the last thing she needed while working on this story!

"Don't cry for me, Springs Ve-*ro*-na . . . ," Jessica sang. She danced around in front of Isabella, who was grinning from ear to ear. "The truth is . . . um, I forgot the next part."

She ran to the full-length mirror in Nick's bedroom and twirled in circles, admiring her new 1940s style frock. The dark green checks brought out the green in her aquamarine eyes.

"Come on, Evita," Isabella called out playfully from the black leather couch. "It's getting late, and we still have work to do." Isabella had been helping her play dress up with her new undercover outfits since they'd arrived at Nick's apartment a half hour before.

Jessica shimmied across the parquet floor on her six-inch heels. "I feel like dancing a tango!"

Isabella snickered. "You'll have to wait until your boyfriend gets home. After all the vintage clothing stores we hit today, I couldn't dance a two-step."

Jessica swooped down on her friend. "Nick's working the night shift at the station. You'll have to be my hot Latina partner."

Isabella squealed and crossed her arms over her ribbed top. "No way! If I move another muscle, I'll collapse."

Jessica dropped down next to her. "All right, darling," she said with a heavy accent. "I'll take pity on you this time, but tomorrow night we samba till dawn!"

Isabella giggled and adjusted the cuff on Jessica's sleeve. "This dress really is the best one so far. With a scarf around your head and dark sunglasses, no one would ever guess you're not from Argentina."

Jessica stood up, humming another song from the movie soundtrack of *Evita*. She reached down into the suitcase and pulled out the next dress. "What do you think of this one?" she asked. She held the silvery-blue frock up to her chest. "Do you think it looks a little threadbare?" She handed it to Isabella.

"Hmmm," Isabella murmured, studying the shiny material near the waist. "A little. But I think I can fix it." She draped the dress across the back of the couch and reached down into Jessica's suitcase. "Voila!" She pulled out another one of their purchases—a skinny faux alligator skin belt. "This will cover the spot. Plus it matches those heels perfectly."

"Izzy, you're a genius," Jessica pronounced. She gave her a big hug. "I don't know what I'd do without you. How did you know about all those great vintage clothing stores anyway?"

Isabella smiled and ran a slender hand through her glossy black tresses. "When you love clothes as much as I do, but only get a limited wardrobe allowance, you learn these tricks pretty quickly."

Jessica nodded. "You always do look fantastic."

Isabella's porcelain-white cheeks blushed rosy. "Enough about me. Let's get these dresses hung up so the wrinkles come out."

Jessica opened the door to Nick's hall closet and pushed his two sports coats aside. The empty wooden hanger was where he hung his leather jacket. *I wish Nick was here,* she thought with a flash of tenderness. She missed him when he worked nights—even when she was with friends.

But that will all be over soon, she told herself as she put the dresses on hangers. *If this assignment goes well, I should be able to work undercover with him on every job!*

Isabella yawned loudly and dangled her car keys. "I'm going to head out, Jess," she said exhaustedly. "*Some* of us have classes tomorrow, you know."

Jessica whipped around and glanced at Nick's

wall clock. "Midnight already? Sorry, Iz. I guess it's too late for you to see Danny."

Isabella shrugged. "That's OK. He knew I was going shopping with you. He probably didn't expect to see me for a week."

Jessica started to laugh, but suddenly felt a tightening in her jaw. "You didn't tell him *why* we were going shopping, did you?" If word spread around SVU that she was trying to perfect an Eva Peron look, then even a *total* transformation wouldn't be enough. Everyone would know it was Jessica under all those clothes and makeup—and then she wouldn't stand a chance of making it undercover.

Isabella shook her head, covering another yawn with her hand. "Just told him it was a girls' day out."

Jessica let out a loud rush of breath. "Thank goodness." She grabbed Isabella's hand. "Please don't tell anybody about this, especially not Danny, and *special*-especially not Lila. OK? Swear to it?"

"Sure," Isabella promised. "Don't worry. But just out of curiosity, why *not* Danny? He'd *never* go to the Verona Springs Country Club."

"It's not your boyfriend," Jessica sighed. "It's his *roommate*. Tom's a supersnoop. If he ever found out I was up there with Nick in disguise, he might want to investigate why. Or he might spill the beans to Liz, who would jump on me in a second. Nick would never forgive me for blowing this case."

Isabella nodded and crossed her heart. "Let me know how you make out," she called from the door.

Jessica waved good-bye to her friend, but still felt slightly uneasy. How could she expect Isabella to keep quiet when she couldn't herself?

Oh well, Jessica thought, *there's nothing I can do about it now. Except make this transformation as radical as I can, and hope that no one will recognize me no matter what!*

She reached into her suitcase and pulled out her large makeup bag before heading into the bathroom. She had two tricks up her sleeve that even Isabella didn't know about.

Jessica removed her tweezers from the side pocket of the bag and bent in close to the mirror. With a swift hand, she began pruning her eyebrows down to size for the perfect Evita look.

"Ow," she yelped as the final pluck was completed. She raised her new pencil-thin eyebrows and examined them. "Perfect," she purred. She could feel a song starting up again in her head. But she stifled the urge to dance. She had one more thing to do.

With a gulp, she turned back to her makeup bag and pulled out a bottle of semi-permanent black hair dye. "Good-bye, Jessica Wakefield," she murmured. "*Hola,* Perdita del Mar!"

Chapter Nine

"What a drag." Bruce yawned loudly and glanced around the empty patio of the Verona Springs Country Club. The early Tuesday morning sun was shimmering brightly on the still water in the pool. The outdoor furniture was stacked neatly in the far corner of the terrace and the patio bar was closed. "Never mind a cup of coffee. We can't even get a seat at this hour," he exclaimed.

Lila shivered a little in her black and white polka-dot halter dress. "I'm sure they'll be opening up soon." She glanced at her slim Gucci watch. "It's almost eight."

Bruce groaned and swung his tennis bag lightly by his side. "And what are we supposed to do until then?" He leaned against the railing encircling the deck, wincing when he discovered that it was covered with early morning dew. "Oh great," he complained. "Now my tennis shorts are drenched."

Lila rolled her eyes. "It's just water. It'll dry." She pulled a thin white sweater from her leather bag and draped it across her bare shoulders.

"I should have stayed in bed," he grumbled. Before Lila's seven A.M. phone call, he'd been having a great dream about trouncing Paul and Bunny on the tennis court.

Lila pursed her lips. "You promised. I have a lot of organizational work to do before today's tournament, and I could really use your support."

Bruce sighed. Becoming a member of the exclusive VIP group of the Club was starting to appeal to him less and less. *But it matters to Lila,* he reminded himself. *And since I've already made myself the buffoon of the place, I might as well go along. My status can only improve—it sure can't fall any farther.*

A waiter appeared and started toward them carrying a striped deck chair. But when he got close enough to recognize Bruce, he grinned and veered to the other side of the patio.

"What was that all about?" Lila asked.

Bruce shook his head. "Nothing." He watched the waiter join two of his colleagues and open up the patio bar. They looked over at Bruce and broke into laughter.

"There, Bruce," Lila said sweetly. She pointed to the edge of the patio where the grinning waiter had placed the chair. "Now you've got a seat. And I've got to run."

"What do you mean, 'run'?" Bruce asked. "I thought you wanted me to help you."

Lila patted his arm. "I *do,* honey. Your driving me up here was a *big* help. But now I've got to get to *work.*"

Bruce's mouth dropped open. "Are you *serious?* You only dragged me out of bed for a *lift?* What am I going to do now while the rest of the world sleeps?"

Lila shrugged, a small giggle escaping from between her lips. "Stay out of trouble?"

"Very funny," Bruce scowled. "Trouble should be all too easy to avoid, since there isn't another person around for miles."

Lila smirked. "You could talk to the staff."

Bruce gave her a dark look. Out of the corner of his eye he could see one of the waiters recreating some of the more embarrassing moves he'd made in their loss to Bunny and Paul. "I can't believe you're doing this to me," he complained. "Everyone thinks I'm a klutz *and* I have nothing to do."

Lila stood on her tiptoes and kissed him on the forehead. "I'll come back in a few hours and check on you. Until then you'll just have to amuse yourself." Then she disappeared into the yellow clubhouse.

Bruce dropped his tennis bag onto the wooden deck and had just sunk down into the striped chair when Paul came lumbering around the corner from the garden. "Patman, old sod," he called. He had his racket and was dressed in tennis whites. These shorts were even baggier than the ones he'd been wearing yesterday. The cuffs hung down well below his knees.

Bruce watched as the waiters scattered to the far corners of the patio as Paul approached.

"Fancy a game?" Paul asked. "Bunny and I aren't scheduled to play the second round of the tournament until this afternoon. Thought I'd get in some practice shots."

Bruce jumped from his seat. *Would I ever!* he thought. But there was no use playing if Lila and Bunny were going to be involved. That would only mean another humiliating defeat—at Bruce's own hands. "Where's Bunny?" he asked.

"Don't know what the old girl is up to this morning," Paul responded. He stumbled as he shifted his weight from one foot to the other, but caught himself before he went tumbling down the stairs. "I thought we could do this man to man—without the ladies."

Bruce felt himself begin to break out into a huge grin. He quickly rubbed a hand over his chin to hide it. "Sure, Paul," he agreed, nonchalantly. "Let me get my gear."

He bent down to pick up his tennis bag, his spirits soaring. *All right!* he bellowed silently. *Ego repair, here I come. Without Lila around to intervene, I'm going to stomp this loser and win back my self-respect!*

* * *

"Nick!" Jessica called. "I'm over here." She smiled as she watched her boyfriend move across the tiled floor of The Mug Shot diner like a panther in the jungle—stealthy and sexy in his leather jacket and torn blue jeans.

He slid into the red vinyl booth across from her, his forest green eyes tired but beaming with pleasure. "You look fantastic."

Jessica grinned and raised her fashionably thick-rimmed sunglasses. "So do you," she purred. "You're quite a sight for sore eyes. I missed you last night."

Nick gave her a crooked smile. "Don't get any ideas. This is strictly business." He called out to the waitress for two more coffees.

Jessica laughed and let her glasses slide back down to her nose. "So how do you like Perdita del Mar from Argentina?" she asked, putting on her heavy Latin accent.

Nick shook his head in apparent awe. "Unbelievable. Stand up, honey. Let's get the whole look."

Jessica stood and did a slow walk for him up and down on her stilettos. She giggled as the place erupted into catcalls and whistles from the other early morning diners.

"Whew!" Nick grinned, running a hand through his dark, tousled hair. "It's a good thing we're inside, or you'd be stopping traffic."

The waitress appeared and set two steaming mugs on the table.

Jessica laughed and stopped in front of the mirrored wall by the cashier to adjust her light blue chiffon scarf. It had slipped from her newly-dyed black hair, the curls of which were piled elaborately atop her head. She tucked a loose strand behind her ear and ran her hands down her hips, smoothing the tailored line of her blue-flowered, 1940s style dress. "How are my seams?" she called to Nick.

He gulped as his eyes traveled the length of her calves. "Perfect. But where did you find old fashioned stockings like that in this day and age?"

"That was easy," she said with a mischievous smile. "Finding an old garter belt was the hard part." She laughed as Nick's jaw dropped. "Down, boy," she giggled. "They're just retro pantyhose." She lifted her dark glasses again and winked. "Oooh, I shouldn't be telling you my trade secrets. Let's just say I'm a master of disguise!" She shimmied toward him, her thick golden cuff bracelets catching the light.

"That's for sure," Nick agreed, raising his mug of coffee in a mock toast. "Perdita del Mar, you look like a million bucks."

Jessica giggled and took her seat at the booth across from him. "But now that I'm ready to steer you through the rocky shoals of country club life, we have to do something about *your* look."

"What do you mean?" Nick asked, slightly taken aback. "I've got my disguise down. When we get back to my apartment, I'll shave and change into the clothes I was wearing yesterday."

"Uh—excuse me?" Jessica crinkled her nose. "I don't *think* so."

Nick frowned and took a sip of his coffee. "I thought I looked pretty good. *You* didn't recognize me."

Jessica smiled sweetly. "You looked like a nerd. A very handsome, well-built nerd, but a nerd nonetheless."

"I worked hard on that outfit."

Jessica let out a hoot of laughter but quickly bit her lip when she saw his hurt look. "I know, darling." She took his hand in hers. "Maybe you can use it if we ever have to infiltrate a computer gadget convention. But no respectable country club would ever let you through the front gate looking like that."

Nick groaned. "So what am I going to do?"

Jessica squeezed his hand. "Don't worry. In case you hadn't noticed, makeover is practically my middle name!"

"Whew, old chum," Paul panted, wiping sweat from his brow. "Showing great form."

Bruce rolled his eyes as Paul trotted over to the side of the tennis court and reached for his bottle of water. *Form nothing,* he thought. *I could have stood in place and* still *won that set!*

He'd soundly beaten Paul in six straight games to take the first set—breaking Paul's serve in three of them! Bruce had barely restrained himself from shouting advice after Paul hit his first four serves into the net—a double-double-fault. Even those shots that Bruce had accidentally plopped down the middle of the court had Paul swinging wildly.

Bruce wandered over to where Paul was struggling with the screw cap on his water bottle. "Need help?" he asked, the sarcasm practically dripping from his voice.

"No thanks. I think I've got it," Paul replied seriously.

Man, this guy's dense, Bruce thought. *He doesn't even know when I'm ribbing him.*

"Whoa," Paul cried. The plastic top went flying off. In his mania he squeezed the bottle, squirting a geyser of water squarely in Bruce's face, drenching his shirt. "Whoops! I guess it got away from me."

"I guess it did," Bruce growled.

Paul gave a little laugh. "Let's hope that cools you off."

Hardly, Bruce thought furiously. He wiped his face with his towel. *He* hadn't broken a sweat.

Paul fumbled toward him with his towel to help blot off the water.

"That's OK," Bruce cried, taking a leap backwards. If he'd learned anything over the past few days, it was not to let Paul anywhere near him.

Paul looked downcast. "Sorry, dear chap. I feel really terrible about this."

Bruce shook his head. "It'll dry during the next set."

"No, really. I want to make it up to you."

Bruce shrugged. What could Paul possibly do to make it up to him? He had bruises up and down his body from where Paul had collided into him yesterday. Everyone at the country club thought he was a doofus. And now he was soaking wet. "Let's just play." *At least that way,* Bruce thought, *I can exact my revenge by wiping up the court with you.*

"OK," Paul agreed, lumbering back to his side of the tennis court. "But I still feel terrible about your shirt. Maybe we can put a little wager on this next set?"

Ka-ching! Bruce's ears rang like a cash register. *Wager! I'll make out like a bandit!* "Um, OK, if you'd like . . . ."

Paul smiled. "More like if *you* do, old stick. Remember, I beat you yesterday."

Bruce felt his eyes blazing and his grip tightened on his tennis racket. "Yes, of course," he agreed through his clenched jaw. *But that's the last match you'll ever win from me,* he amended fiercely. "Ten dollars a game sound OK?"

Paul grinned. "Fine by me. I'll try not to take too many games off you!"

Hit me with your best shot, Bruce thought, hiding a smirk. *This is going to be like taking candy from a baby!*

"Hey Carlos," Tom called with a smile. "Carlos!" But the friendly waiter he'd spoken to the previous day apparently hadn't heard him. Tom watched from his seat in the employees' lounge as Carlos approached two Latino coworkers. Both were wearing white chef's hats and aprons. Carlos spoke to them quickly and in a low voice. Too low and fast for Tom to have picked up—even if his Spanish had been up to the challenge.

After a few moments, each chef reached into his pocket and pulled out some money. One of the men peeled off two bills and handed them to Carlos, but Carlos shook his head and pointed to the palm of his hand. Tom watched as the man resignedly handed over the rest of the bills he was holding. The second man did likewise.

Tom frowned. "What's that about?" he mumbled. "Do those guys owe Carlos money?" Tom felt conspicuous staring at them, so he glanced at his watch. It was nearly nine A.M., and Dana would be bounding through the front door of the employees' lounge any second to prepare for a mid-morning concerto on the great lawn. Tom smiled, thinking how nice it was to have someone bursting to see him.

He adjusted the collar of his white button-down shirt and let his eyes wander around the brightly lit room. A few more employees had arrived and were storing their bags and street shoes in their lockers.

Tom turned back to watching Carlos. He'd moved on to another group of employees—three women in khaki skirts and white polos who were sipping their morning coffee at the main table in the middle of the room.

A prickly feeling of uneasiness came over Tom as he watched the women—with apparent reluctance—open up their pocketbooks and hand money over to Carlos.

Tom scratched his head. Unless Carlos acted as the local bank, he sure was collecting a lot of debts. Tom stood up and wandered over to him. "Hey, Carlos, what are you doing?" he asked.

Carlos jumped up and stuffed the last wad of bills into his front pocket. "Tom, amigo . . . you'll give someone a heart attack doing that." He placed his hand on his chest and made patting motions.

Tom shrugged, trying to look contrite and innocently nosy at the same time. "Sorry. I saw you over here . . . ," he began brightly. But then he stopped. What exactly *was* it that he'd seen?

Carlos took him by the arm and led him a short distance away from the rest of the employees. "Ah, taking donations," he filled in, smoothly finishing

Tom's implied question. "Maria Martinez, a former employee, is getting married. It's customary for coworkers to give a cash gift."

Tom smiled. "That's nice . . . though some of your fellow coworkers didn't look too happy about it."

Carlos nodded. "Yes, some people can be real 'tightwads' as you say. They forget what it's like to be young and struggling. When all that you have is your love."

Tom gulped. He remembered that feeling all too well. So many times in the past, he'd had to struggle to take Elizabeth anywhere nice. She'd never seemed to mind. But still, it had hurt Tom's pride that he wasn't able to give the girl he loved everything he felt she deserved. Of course all that had been before George Conroy and his deep pockets came along.

Tom pulled out his wallet. "I'd like to contribute," he offered, taking out a ten-dollar bill.

"Oh, no," Carlos protested, holding up his hand. "You don't even know Maria. You don't work here. You're a member."

"That's OK," Tom replied. "I know what it's like to be poor and in love." He took his pen out of his pocket. "How do you say 'good luck' in Spanish?"

Carlos smiled. *"Buena suerte."*

Tom wrote the words on the corner of the bill in large letters and handed it to Carlos. "I hope this brings her a very happy life."

"Thanks, amigo," Carlos said, with a nervous laugh. "I'm sure it will."

"No way," Jessica gasped, laughter convulsing her lithe body. She grabbed one of Nick's throw pillows and covered her face with it. "I'm *telling* you," she squeaked. "If they see you dressed like *that,* they'll have the country club guards escort you out the front gates—on your head!"

"What's the problem?" Nick said testily, stamping his foot on the living room floor. His high-water pant legs flapped around his ankles.

Jessica bit back a fresh batch of giggles. She leapt from the couch and walked a wide circle around him, surveying Nick from every angle. "Those pants have *got* to go," she announced finally.

Nick frowned. "Why? You said no jeans. These aren't jeans. They're chinos. I saw *lots* of guys there wearing chinos the other day. And *don't* tell me to wear a suit either. I wore a suit last time, and everyone treated me like I was invisible. It's pretty casual there, especially for guys."

"*Casual,* yeah." Jessica rolled her eyes and giggled. "*Casual* and *comfortable* and *fashionable,* Nick. I bet most of the guys there are wearing stuff that's loose and baggy. These pants are about five sizes too small for you! Plus they're so short, your ankles show! And what on Earth is that on your *feet?*"

Nick looked down. "Converse high-tops. They're *casual* and *comfortable* and *fashionable*."

"Maybe in another lifetime." Jessica snorted. "But for the country club scene, your choices are limited—tennis sneakers, loafers, or deck shoes."

"Deck shoes!" Nick exclaimed, putting his hands up to his neck as if he were choking. "That's wimp wear of the worst kind!"

Jessica gave Nick's physique a quick visual appraisal. His arm muscles were practically bursting through the sleeves of his white button-down shirt. "Nick, no one would *ever* think you were a wimp. And with the right trousers, deck shoes can look *rah-thah dah*-shing."

Nick groaned and fell back onto the couch. "I'm not cut out for this preppy stuff."

Jessica raised one razor-thin eyebrow. "That's because you're not dressed preppily *enough*. Those clothes make you look more like sergeant of the Geek Patrol."

Nick threw up his hands. "What's the difference?"

Jessica bounced up and down in exasperation. "The difference between entrance to the most exclusive country club in Southern California—and a free pass to a Saturday night study session at the library!"

"It's all the same to me," Nick grumbled.

Jessica bent over the arm of the couch and planted a gentle series of kisses along his jawbone.

"That's because your sense of style is so *different*—so dangerous and sexy."

Nick reached out and pulled her into his lap. "Go on," he murmured.

She laughed and ran her fingers along his strong, muscular shoulders. "Those other guys can only *dream* about having a body like yours."

"So why don't I go like me?"

"Hmmm," Jessica whispered, nibbling his ear. "You'd stick out like a sore thumb."

"What?" Nick cried, upending her as he got to his feet abruptly.

Jessica quickly recovered herself, patting her elaborate hairdo back into place and smoothing down her flowered dress. "Not in a bad way. It's just that country club guys all wear a certain uniform. They don't trust outsiders. If we're going to infiltrate this place, we've got to get them to think you're one of them."

"And how am I supposed to do that?" Nick grumbled.

"Come on," Jessica softly admonished him. "Let's go look through your closet." She stood up, took him by the hand, and led him into the bedroom.

Nick took a seat on the edge of the bed, staring at her glumly. "You can give it a try, but this was the only outfit I could come up with."

"Trust me, Nick. And *no sulking* either." Jessica tried to look him over without bursting into giggles again. "Well, I have to admit, you *did* pick out a decent shirt."

"But that's all, right?"

Jessica wrinkled her nose. "I'm afraid so. Also, you've got to shave and wash that goo out of your hair. Plus I'm going to have to trim it."

Nick jumped up from the bed. "Now *that's* where I draw the line!"

"Nick," Jessica scolded him. "You're on *my* territory now. But if you can get your waves to behave without a can of grease, then I won't have to cut anything."

Nick groaned and disappeared into the bathroom.

While Nick was rinsing his hair, Jessica rummaged through his closets and drawers. Sure enough, she found nothing but a wrinkled tweed blazer and a dusty pair of leather dress shoes. "Pants, pants," she chanted. "Where're the pants?"

Her fingers crossed for luck, Jessica peered under the bed. She found a dust-bunny-covered gift box there. "Aha!" she shouted, pulling out the box and opening it. Three pairs of casual drcss slacks were inside—one olive, one khaki, one navy—the tags still attached. A card lay on top. It read To Nicky—Happy Birthday, Love Mom and Dad.

"Nicky." Jessica snorted. *No wonder he hid these under his bed and forgot about them,* she noted. *They're totally not his style!*

Nick came out of the bathroom, a towel wrapped around his waist, beads of water glistening on his bare chest.

"No fair," Jessica said throatily, averting her eyes from his gorgeous body. "You're trying to distract me, *Nicky*."

"*Don't* call me that." Nick grabbed the three pairs of casual slacks from her hands. "Where in the world did you find *these?*"

"Under your bed. My powers of investigation are flawless."

He looked over the rest of the clothing she'd picked out for him and nodded approvingly. "I'll slip these on before your face turns permanently red." He gestured to the towel which encircled his hips and left little to the imagination. "Now, if you'll *excuse* me . . . "

Jessica let out a sigh and fanned herself with her hands as she scooted out into the living room.

A few minutes later, Nick presented himself.

Jessica's mouth dropped open. With his close shaven face, neatly combed and parted hair, khaki slacks, and white shirt, Nick looked like he'd just stepped off the pages of a fifties guide to style. He'd polished the black leather shoes, and he'd obviously let the tweed blazer sit in the steam-filled bathroom while he'd gotten ready; the wrinkles were barely visible.

"I don't believe it," she cried. "You're a total prepster!"

Nick laughed. "No need to look so surprised, Jess. It's still me, you know."

"Yes . . . a bit *too* much you." Jessica paused thoughtfully before stumbling to her suitcase. She pulled out a pair of men's vintage round-rimmed glasses. "Try these on."

After giving her a reluctant squint, Nick put on the glasses and instantly became unrecognizable.

"Chip!" Jessica dubbed him, ignoring the gagging noises he made. "Oh, Chip, *dah*-ling, I think we've *done* it!"

Chapter Ten

"I sure hope the manager's in a talkative mood," Elizabeth murmured to herself. She knocked lightly on the door to the club manager's office, straining to make sense of the indistinct sounds she could hear from within.

She shifted her feet uneasily and glanced down the dark, highly polished wood hallway. Verona Springs's executive office suite oozed privilege and power and made her feel slightly uncomfortable.

She knocked again, more loudly this time, and fished her reporter's notebook from her large shoulder bag. "As long as they think I'm here for a fluff story," she told herself calmly, "I'll be fine." Still no one called for her to enter.

Elizabeth glanced at her watch. Scott had made the appointment for ten A.M. and it was a little before that now. *Maybe the manager's gone off to get a cup of coffee,* she thought. *No.* She could definitely hear voices inside.

Elizabeth pushed gently against the door. It swung open into a small reception area dominated by an unoccupied desk.

Elizabeth stepped inside. *There's no reason why I can't wait in the reception area,* she reasoned. The muffled voices she'd heard before were now much clearer. Obviously the receptionist and manager were discussing something inside.

"Oh, one more thing," a woman's high-pitched voice said. "Did we ever get an address for Manuel Coimbra?"

"Who was that?" the manager's deep baritone asked.

"He was the busboy that left suddenly . . . what was it, a week? Two weeks ago? You remember, he didn't give notice."

"Oh, right, Coimbra. Why? Has there been some trouble?"

Elizabeth heard a rustling of paper. "No, nothing like that," the receptionist responded. "But we've received some more letters addressed to him. Not that I expect he would ever read them, since he barely spoke English."

"Hmmm," the manager replied. "Leave them with the rest of his mail."

Elizabeth's ears were burning. Was it just an odd coincidence, or did this Manuel Coimbra's disappearance have something to do with the drowning? She jotted the name down in the back of her reporter's notebook.

The receptionist stepped out of the manager's office and started when she saw Elizabeth. Her hand flew to her mouth. "Oh," she cried. "I didn't know anyone was here."

I'm sure you didn't, Elizabeth thought suspiciously. She smiled and put on her best imitation bubbly college girl act. "The door was open, so I just came in. I hope you don't mind but, I mean, hallways are *so* drafty. If you want I'll go outside and knock again."

The receptionist rolled her icy blue eyes behind her wire-rimmed glasses and motioned for Elizabeth to take a seat. "You must be the society reporter from the *Gazette*. Mr. Pendleton will be with you shortly."

Elizabeth sat down and pretended to fussily arrange the hem of her olive green sundress. But all the time she was keeping careful watch as the receptionist removed a manila envelope from beneath a fat stack of papers on her desk. She put several pieces of mail inside it. Suddenly the woman's eyes flashed at Elizabeth.

Elizabeth quickly dropped her gaze and swallowed a gasp. *Is she trying to hide that envelope from me?* she thought excitedly. She dared not look. Instead she kept her attention firmly on fiddling with the strap of her leather sandal.

"There," she murmured, half-aloud, as if

putting her own shoes on each morning was a recently acquired ability. Then slowly, ever so slowly, she allowed her gaze to travel back to the desk.

The manila envelope was gone! She ran her eyes around the woman's desk frantically. But the place where it had previously been now held only papers.

As she stared, Elizabeth could feel the woman's cold eyes studying her. Elizabeth flashed her most benign smile. The last thing she wanted was to awaken this woman's suspicion, though the woman had surely awoken hers.

The receptionist scowled back at her and punched a button on her intercom. "The reporter girl is here to see you."

Mr. Pendleton's voice came back in a crackle. "Send her in."

"Thanks much!" Elizabeth simpered as she started for the manager's door. She gave one last quick glance behind the desk as she walked past.

Bingo! Elizabeth thought. Peeking out of the lower drawer of the desk was a corner of the manila envelope. *If I can't get any satisfactory information from the manager, maybe I can get some answers* there.

Smash! Another perfect ace came sizzling off Bruce's racket. "That makes it three games in a row," Bruce blurted excitedly. "Looks like you owe me thirty dollars."

Paul stumbled up to the net. "Bruce," he panted through jerky, shallow gasps, "you're really giving me a workout today."

Bruce beamed. *A drubbing is more like it,* he thought, his ego rapidly pumping back up to its original size. *I just wish there were people around to witness this!*

"I don't know what's with me today," Paul continued. He wandered over to the side of the tennis court and slumped down onto the wooden bench. "I was playing so well yesterday."

Bruce pretended to wipe sweat from his face to cover a grin. *Yesterday was a joke,* Bruce thought. *Today I'm playing to clobber you.*

Paul sighed and wiped a towel across his face. "Hey, I know what'll make this game *reeeally* exciting! Let's play the rest of this set at a *hundred* dollars a game!"

Bruce gulped. "That's crazy!" he exclaimed. Sure he wanted to show Paul up, but he didn't want to *rob* him.

Paul jumped to his feet. "No, I'm serious. I'm sure that if I have enough riding on a game, it'll motivate me to play better. Like yesterday, when Bun-bun and I advanced to the second round of the tournament."

Bruce made a face. "That's still a lot of cash."

"Oh, be a sport. It's only money." Paul attempted to twirl his racket but ended up flinging it across the court. "Whoops!" He walked over to retrieve it and then turned and looked over his shoulder at Bruce. "You can cover it if your luck runs out."

My luck? Bruce thought furiously. *That's* skill! Whatever misgivings he had about fleecing Paul vanished instantly. He stalked off to his side of the tennis court. If this joker still thought he was the superior player after the trouncing he'd taken over the last three games, so be it. He'd take him for every dime he had! "You're on!" Bruce cried.

"Good," Paul smiled. He pulled a ball from his pocket and bounced it on the court. "And since you seem so into it, how about if we raise it to two hundred a game?"

Bruce felt the color drain out of his face. "Two hundred?" *This guy must have money to burn,* he thought. "That's a little steep, don't you think?"

Paul gave him a reptilian smile. "Can't handle it? Hmmm . . . maybe the Verona Springs Country Club is too expensive for your blood."

Bruce narrowed his eyes. *Hardly,* he thought. He came from one of the richest families in Sweet Valley. He could easily match Paul dollar for dollar. But two hundred a game—Bruce somehow didn't feel right about taking Paul for that much, regardless of how furious he was. "I was thinking of *you,*" he retorted.

Paul laughed and waved his concern away. "I don't plan to lose."

Bruce almost gagged. *Fat chance,* he thought,

getting into his receiver's crouch. *But if he insists on throwing away his money, fine, I won't stop him. Maybe this will teach him a lesson about gambling. And I'll have a nice chunk of this arrogant jerk's money to donate to a worthy charity.*

"Ready," Bruce called. And Paul raised his racket, tossing the first ball in the air for his serve.

"This way, please," the handsome Latino waiter intoned. He began leading Jessica and Nick to a table at the edge of the patio.

"That will *not* do," Jessica mumbled. For her act to work, she needed to be the center of attention. Jessica raised her voice by a good ten decibels. "Dar-*leeng!*" she cried, pulling no punches with her Perdita del Mar accent. "*Thees* table *ees* totally *ahn*-acceptable. I am Perdita del Mar of the Argentina del Mars. I *inseest* we *seet* in the *meeddle* of the *rrroom!*"

The waiter blushed, and Nick looked equally embarrassed. But from behind her dark sunglasses, Jessica saw that her little ploy was working wonderfully. Everyone dining on the terrace had looked up at them, and most members of the Verona Springs Country Club were subtly nodding their approval as the waiter hastily seated them in the middle of the patio before rushing off to find menus.

Jessica leaned in close to Nick, pretending to adjust his tie. "Snobs love snobbery," she whispered.

"Now they'll think we're one of them." She sat back, smiled, and placed her faux alligator-skin bag on the table.

The waiter returned and gingerly handed them their menus.

Nick let out a low whistle, and Jessica immediately discovered why. The cheapest thing on the lunch menu was a side salad, and that cost about as much as Nick made in a day.

"Shhh," Jessica warned. "We have an expense account, remember."

Nick narrowed his jade-green eyes. "Well, at least if we can't find new evidence about the murder, we can close down the club for highway robbery."

Jessica giggled and then returned to her Evita act. She tossed the menu aside in a huff. "What *are* these kinds of foods which I am finding in this . . . how do you say . . . *may-noo?*"

"Menu," Nick pronounced quietly.

"Filet mignon and lobster? *Ooof!*" Jessica raged on. "No beluga caviar? No quail eggs? How is an heiress supposed to eat? *Ay,* I'll *starve* from this peasant food."

"Muffin," Nick cried, slipping into his role as Chip. "*Please* don't concern yourself. I'm sure they must have *one* decent chef on staff to whip you up what you need."

"I am not sure of that which you say." Jessica sniffed, acting heartbroken. "In Argentina, the chefs, they *live* to please us. *This* menu—she has no *heart.*"

The waiter slunk by. "Um, *señorita,* the head chef has informed me that he would be honored to create for you anything you would like."

Jessica smiled widely. Obviously word had gone out that Perdita del Mar was a personage of distinction. "But of course," she replied. "Tell him we'll begin with oysters on the half shell, followed by two bowls of gazpacho and plenty of polenta, *por favor.*"

As soon as the waiter turned, Nick grabbed her hand. "What did you order, exactly?"

Jessica laughed. "Don't worry. It's just spicy tomato soup with corn bread."

Nick let out a sigh of relief. "Good. I was afraid you were going to have me eating raw beef and chicken kidneys to prove I was preppy."

Jessica giggled. Within minutes the food was before them.

Nick grabbed a spoon and started for his soup.

"The oysters first," Jessica whispered out of the side of her mouth. After all the attention they'd attracted, it just wouldn't do to slip up in the etiquette department with all eyes trained on them.

"Why?" Nick whispered back. "I don't want my soup to get cold."

Jessica gave a small shake of her head, careful not to disturb the blue chiffon scarf that was covering her elaborate hairdo. "It's already cold."

"Ohhh," Nick complained. He reached for the little fork that came with the oysters and started to pluck the mollusk out of its shell.

"No," Jessica whispered again. "Loosen the oyster, and *then* pick up the shell." She demonstrated by daintily tipping the shell and letting the oyster slip into her mouth.

Nick groaned. "On most jobs all I have to do is belly up to the bar and order a beer."

Jessica smiled. "But all you get to eat *there* are stale peanuts."

Nick finished his half-dozen oysters. "Not bad," he admitted.

"Told you so," she teased.

After they finished their lunch, Jessica pushed her plate away. Immediately the waiter was at their side to clear away their dishes.

"Señor," Jessica inquired loudly, "where may I find the polo ponies?"

The waiter's dark eyes widened. "I'm sorry, *señorita,* but the Verona Springs Country Club doesn't have polo ponies."

"No polo ponies?" she gasped, clutching a hand to her chest. "*No polo ponies!* Where I come from, you would not dare to even call yourself a *club!*"

"Lo siento, señorita. Lo siento mucho." The waiter backed away full of apologies, his arms laden with the tray full of dishes.

"I am *appalled,*" Jessica shrilled. "What shall

we do to occupy our time in this . . . how do you say . . . *backwater establishment?*"

Nick gave her a subtle nod and Jessica shifted her glance sideways. Sure enough her best friend, Lila, along with an extremely snobby-looking couple, were starting toward them.

"We've got their attention now," Jessica whispered, adjusting her thick, golden cuff bracelets. "It's only a matter of time before they make us the toast of the town . . . and we make them spill all their secrets!"

"That was a big waste of time," Elizabeth muttered as she stepped out of the manager's office. "I learned absolutely nothing." Whenever she'd tried to direct their conversation to possible improprieties on the club grounds, the manager would suddenly have to make a phone call. And then as soon as he was off the call, he'd go back to rambling on about how moneyed and respectable all the club members were!

Either I'm slipping up as an investigative reporter, she thought, *or he's one artful dodger. And if that's the case, then he must be in this up to his neck.*

"But what is *this?*" she murmured in response to her own thoughts. "A cover-up? A murder? Both? What is *this?*" One thing was for sure—she needed more information.

Elizabeth closed the manager's door behind

her and readied her empty-headed smile for the receptionist's benefit. But as she turned to deliver some parting pleasantries, she realized the receptionist wasn't there at all. Apparently she'd headed off to another part of the executive office suite.

"Hmmm," Elizabeth murmured, a devious thought taking shape in her mind. *Should I take the envelope?* she wondered.

Liz! her voice of reason admonished her. *Fooling with mail is a federal offense!*

But then in her mind's eye she pictured her competitor—Tom Watts. If she left this interview now, empty-handed, she was no further along in the investigation than before. If Tom arranged to meet with the club manager, he could come out ahead. She chewed on her bottom lip worriedly. She'd never done anything as reckless as steal mail.

Suddenly she heard the distinctive click of high heels on the wooden floor outside the office. "The receptionist!" Elizabeth gasped. From the rapid sound of the footsteps, she was making good time.

Elizabeth's blue-green eyes darted around the room. It was now or never. But how could she? Taking that mail would be theft, plain and simple.

The footsteps were getting louder now. Any second and the secretary was going to reach the door. "What would Tom do?" Elizabeth cried. Then her mind flashed back to the previous afternoon. She knew exactly what Tom would do—and it had nothing to do with taking mail. Instead

Elizabeth imagined Tom with his arms wrapped around his new girlfriend, Dana, his lips locked passionately with hers.

If I don't take that envelope, she thought furiously, *not only does Tom show me up on the love front, but he'll beat me out on the story as well!*

She stepped quickly behind the desk and snatched the manila envelope from the lower drawer. She was just stuffing it into her shoulder bag when the office door flew open. Elizabeth gasped as the receptionist barreled in, her tiny mouth pursed and her eyes full of menacing suspicion.

Slam! Another ace came sizzling over the net. Only this time, the look on Bruce's face was one of shocked amazement, not gloating triumph. "This can't be happening," he gasped. He shook his head in an attempt to clear his thoughts and bring reason to what was going on.

Klutzy Paul Krandall, who could barely *walk* without tripping over his own two feet, had just served two aces in a row. Bruce hadn't stood a chance of returning either of the serves. The balls had whipped by him so fast, he'd barely had time to lift his racket.

What's going on here? Bruce thought, flustered. When Paul won their first big-money game, Bruce had blamed it on luck and his own lack of concentration. He'd been lulled into a fantasy about which charity he'd give his winnings to, and how much fun it was going to be bragging around the club about how he'd trounced Paul and made a ton of money. It hadn't mattered all that much. All Bruce had to do was win the next big-money game and he'd be back on top financially.

But so far he hadn't been able to so much as get his racket on the ball. Paul's playing had improved a thousand percent. No, a *million* percent. Now it was Paul who was barely breaking a sweat and Bruce who was running scared.

"Are you concentrating, Bruce?" Paul called.

Bruce scowled and got down into his receiving crouch. He balanced himself gingerly on the balls of his feet, ready to go to either side depending on where Paul's next serve came down. He watched Paul lift his arm and toss the tennis ball into the air above his head. Something in Paul's movement, a subtle shifting of his torso as his racket began slicing through the air, told Bruce the ball would come down in the left-hand side of the box. Instinctively, Bruce's body started left.

Whiz! The ball tore across the net, clearing it by millimeters. Too late—Bruce realized that the ball was headed to his right after all. He tried to shift direction, but his body was already committed. He twisted his head in time to see Paul's serve hit the far right-hand corner of the receiving box, kicking up a tiny cloud of red clay dust as it did so.

"You've got to pay attention, old man," Paul

laughed. "Here, I'll make this one easier."

"Don't do me any favors," Bruce growled, getting back into his crouch.

Paul served again, except this time Bruce read the shot perfectly. He charged the net and whacked the ball over. Paul had positioned himself at the far left-hand side of the court and was able to make a quick return. But Bruce was getting his form back, he'd stayed close to the net and sure enough, Paul's lob was coming right at him.

"This time I'll show him who's quick," Bruce murmured. He hit the ball with all his might, sending it barreling down the far right side. It was his best shot and practically a guaranteed winner.

But to Bruce's utter amazement, Paul gracefully leapt into the air—pirouetting like a ballerina—and returned the shot. Worse, even though it looked as if Paul had barely tapped the ball with his racket, it came slamming into the deep end of the center of the court, just out of Bruce's reach.

"That's game! But it was a good try," Paul teased, all signs of clumsiness long gone. "Now you're making it fun for me." Paul tossed him a tennis ball to serve. "Let's hope you can keep it up."

"I'll show you," Bruce muttered. He was still ahead three games to two. Now that it was his serve, he'd turn things around and remind Paul he was still no match for Bruce Patman!

But no matter what Bruce did, Paul returned

every shot. Whether Paul was serving or returning, hitting soft or hard, after a few volleys the ball always ended up just out of Bruce's reach.

Bruce started to get a creepy feeling that Paul was mocking him, teasing him with the placement of his shots. Another overhead smash landed neatly inside the boundary line.

"That's five games to three," Paul announced smugly. "One more game for me and this set is *over.*"

"Break," Bruce panted, trudging off the court to collapse on the bench. He grabbed the water bottle from his tennis bag and took a long, thirsty pull.

"Not wearing you out, am I?" Paul scoffed, twirling his racket. This time it stayed confidently in his grip. "With your Olympic triathlon training in the Andes mountains," he drawled sarcastically, "you should be running circles around me."

"I'm fine," Bruce glowered, the sting of his long-ago lie to Bunny returning a thousandfold. He rubbed an imaginary cramp in his leg to buy himself a little more time. "Charley horse," he explained. He swallowed a groan as he forced himself back onto his exhausted feet, every muscle in his body howling in protest.

Paul bounced the ball twice, getting ready to serve, but then stopped and checked his watch. "Umm. I was afraid of this." He looked over at Bruce. "Lunch appointment, old chum. I'm going to have to wrap it up now."

Bruce's mouth dropped open. "You're going to forfeit the last game?"

Paul hooted. "Of *course* not! I just *can't* be bothered to *volley* with you anymore." He got into his serving stance and powered five aces—one after another—right down the line. They zoomed by Bruce at such speeds he barely had time to register them, let alone return them.

Paul laughed and ran to the net. "Set to Krandall! Six games to three. Bad luck for you."

Suddenly Bruce heard the slow, derisive *rat-tat-tat* of clapping hands behind him. He turned to find Bunny, wearing a slinky red halter dress and a satisfied smile. "Very nice," she simpered. She started toward them. "I only wish I'd seen more. But who could have guessed it would be over so soon?"

Paul came around the net and put his arm around her. "Darling, you said twelve-thirty, I strung it out as long as I could."

Bruce felt his stomach sink. Something was rotten here. Very rotten.

I've been hustled! he realized with a start. And that wasn't all. Bunny had obviously arranged this whole thing to get him back for having treated her so poorly the previous summer.

"Let's go eat, Bun-bun. Lunch is on Bruce," Paul laughed. "And dinner, and lunch, and dinner again!"

Bunny tossed back her brown hair. "Bruce,

how sweet of you to try and make up for that one awful date we had," she said through a plastic smile. "But don't you think you've gone a little overboard? I mean, betting on a tennis match? Everyone knows what a lousy player you are. Hopeless. Really hopeless."

Bruce felt his anger rising to the boiling point.

"I mean, yesterday was just *too* funny," Bunny chattered on, her oversized teeth gleaming in the afternoon sun. "And today is even better. How much did you win by, darling?"

"Six games to three," Paul sneered. "Unfortunately, Bruce won his three games while we were still playing for ten dollars a game. My six games were at two hundred each. That makes . . . one thousand, one hundred and seventy dollars!"

Bruce clutched his racket. He wanted to scream. *I'm not paying you a dime!* he thought. *You ripped me off, and you'll get nothing from me.* "Sorry," he told them, his mouth twisted in a grimace, "but I don't carry that kind of cash on me."

"I doubted you did," Paul smirked. "But a check will suffice."

Bruce clenched his teeth. "Who should I make it out to? Hustler and Associates?"

Bunny tittered. "I told you he had a sense of humor."

Paul laughed as well. "How about making the check to cash? That's easy."

Bruce grumbled and grabbed his checkbook from the inside pocket of his tennis bag. Cash, he wrote, practically stabbing the checkbook with his pen. He filled in the amount and handed the check to Paul with narrowed eyes.

Paul took it and showed another one of his serpent-like smiles. "This won't bounce, will it, old stick? I'd hate for it to get around the club."

Bruce blanched. Paul wasn't going to stop, was he? "My money's good. Better than yours."

Paul smiled, the tip of his tongue licking his lips. He folded the check and slipped it into his shirt pocket, patting it lightly. "Buck up, little camper. What goes around, comes around. Now everyone's even."

Not likely, Bruce thought darkly. *The way I treated Bunny is* nothing *compared to this.* He turned away to stuff his towel and sweatbands into his tennis bag. *As far as I'm concerned this spells all out war!*

Chapter Eleven

I can't believe I just did that, Elizabeth cried silently as she hurried out of the executive office suite, thankfully unconfronted by the receptionist. She ran across the great lawn and up onto the patio. "Scott!" she called, spying him standing by the terrace bar.

He waved her over.

"I stole mail!" she tried to tell him, but her breath was coming out in gasps, making her words unintelligible.

Scott smiled and took her arm, smoothly guiding her away from the bar.

"Wait, Scott . . . ," Elizabeth started. But he kept tugging her along.

Of course, she thought, her shaking knees slowly steadying, *he doesn't want me to blurt things out where everyone can hear. He's taking me someplace private.* So it was with shock that she found herself plopped down at a table with Pepper, Anderson, and Lila in the middle of the patio.

What is Scott doing? her mind raged. *We've got to talk!* She tried to catch his eye, but he ignored her, turning his attention to Pepper.

"Now *that's* a lovely outfit," he praised her. "Armani?"

Pepper tittered, toying with the oversized buttons on her tight beige pantsuit. "How can you tell?"

Scott grinned and ran a hand through his blond hair. "You were *made* for Italian fashion."

Pepper fluttered her long, false eyelashes. "Come closer. I love a man with good taste."

Elizabeth rolled her eyes and kicked Scott under the table. Her heart was still in her throat and her stomach was in knots. For all she knew, the receptionist had searched her desk and realized the manila envelope was missing by now. Security could be after her!

Scott moved his leg away and continued to focus on Pepper. "Have you seen the new Zumpanino collection? The new spring colors will go great with your complexion."

Pepper giggled and patted her fake blond hair. "I like to stay in vogue."

"Oh, brother," Elizabeth muttered under her breath. Whatever investigative technique Scott was using was a mystery to her. *If I were still working with Tom,* she thought, *he would have sensed how my heart is pounding, how desperately I need to confer with him.* They would be safely away right now, sorting through the mail—and working through Elizabeth's profound sense of guilt about having stolen it.

Lila leaned across the table. "What's with you, Liz?"

Elizabeth looked up, startled.

Lila raised an inquiring eyebrow. "Do you have diamonds in that bag or something?"

"What?" Elizabeth gasped. Lila was right. She was clutching her shoulder bag as if it were the last life preserver on the *Titanic*. "No," she stammered, quickly relaxing her death grip. But she overdid it, and the bag tumbled to the patio floor. As if in slow motion, her brush, her compact, her reporter's notepad, and lastly the manila envelope came spilling out for the whole world to see. The big white label and the name Coimbra stood out starkly against the yellow background.

After that, everything seemed to speed up. Elizabeth began to dive for her things, but Anderson beat her to it.

"I've got it," he stated, waving her away.

Elizabeth looked on in horror as he picked up each object, the manila envelope last. She felt the strength seeping from her body like sawdust from a rag doll.

Anderson seemed to hesitate, almost weighing each item in his hand. She clutched the side of the table, her top teeth biting down on her lower lip. In another moment he would turn to her, shaking the envelope and accusing her of theft. She would be carted off to jail before she even had a chance to look inside.

Elizabeth felt her heart thud down to her shoes as his cold gray eyes looked over at her. *This is it,* she thought. *I'm a goner.*

But instead, miraculously and without a word—without even a flicker of interest—Anderson handed the fallen articles back to her. She quickly stuffed the contents into her bag, and turned to Lila with a nervous giggle. "No diamonds here," she managed to croak. She immediately looked down, imagining that the word *guilty* was all but stamped across her forehead.

Lila laughed. "I didn't think so." She leaned across the table toward Elizabeth. "One couple canceled out of today's tournament match," she whispered. "Do you think I should ask those two over there to play?"

Elizabeth took a deep breath, still shaky from her near miss, and looked in the direction in which Lila was tilting her head.

Wow, Elizabeth thought, taking in the woman's mysterious Latin air and the man's suave 1950s elegance. *That's one glamorous couple,* she thought. *They look like they just walked off a Hollywood movie set.*

"Sure," Elizabeth mouthed.

Lila turned to the couple. "Excuse me," she said affably. "I'm Lila Fowler. I couldn't help noticing that you're new here. Would you care to join us?"

Elizabeth relaxed slightly as all attention shifted to the good-looking new couple. *Thank heavens!* It would only have been a matter of time before someone at their table noticed that she was about to jump out of her skin. *Now that I'm safely out of the limelight,* she thought, *how am I going to get Scott to get me out of here?*

"We'd love to join you, *conchita,*" Jessica gushed, hoping her accent sounded more Carmen Miranda than Ricky Ricardo. There was no doubt her outfit looked the part. "I am called Perdita del Mar and this is my adorable *hombre,* Cheep," she said, taking the seat being offered by Lila.

"That's *Chip,*" Nick explained, tugging the cuffs of his tweed blazer.

Jessica laughed uproariously and squeezed Nick's cheek, winking at him through her dark glasses. "He is adorable, no?"

Lila introduced them to the other people sitting around the table. Pepper, Anderson, Scott, and lastly Elizabeth.

Elizabeth! Ai-yi-yi! Jessica suddenly felt as if she'd been asked to swallow a giraffe. What in the world was Elizabeth doing there?

Jessica held her breath as she touched Elizabeth's fingers in what she hoped was the way a South American heiress would shake hands. She'd obviously fooled Lila, but her own twin would more than likely be another story entirely.

But Elizabeth barely looked up, giving her an unfocused smile. *I guess she's got a lot on her mind,* Jessica thought, giving her sister a quick once-over. *Lucky for me. Whoo-hoo!*

"Where are you from?" Lila asked brightly.

Jessica smiled, tucking a stray strand of dark hair into her chiffon scarf. "Argentina, the land of diamonds."

"Really?" Anderson asked, adjusting the knot in his silk cravat. "I always thought *Africa* was famous for its diamonds."

Jessica gulped. *This is what I get for not paying more attention in geography,* she thought. "Mmmm, but of course. That's what we *want* everyone to think, *comprende?* We export our diamonds there so that our country . . . she will not be overrun by *cat burglars.*"

"Wow," Pepper squealed. "Anderson, we should fly down there for my engagement ring!"

"Ah, yes," Jessica mused. "Allow me to recommend Buenos Aires, known the world over as the city of *amore.*"

"I thought Paris was the city of love," Scott piped up.

"And I thought *amore* was *Italian,*" Elizabeth murmured, still looking as if she was floating out in space.

"They learned it all from us!" Jessica insisted. From the corner of her eye, she could see Nick turning a pale shade of green. She leaned over and gave him a soft kiss on the cheek. "Don't worry. They're believing everything I say," she whispered into his ear. "As long as Liz stays clueless, we're home free."

Clearing her throat, Jessica sat back with a Cheshire cat grin and surveyed her audience. "And those cute little berets the French wear? We designed those from the wool of our yaks."

"Yaks?" Lila countered, her dark brown eyes widening.

"Another import from Argentina," Jessica laughed. "Everyone wants a piece of our country, but as our most famous actress, Evita, once said, 'we in Argentina live only for love, the sun, and our coconut milk.'"

"Coconut milk?" Anderson asked. "That's big there? I thought Argentina was famous for its beef."

Jessica waved him away. "An old *señora's* myth to attract *hombres* for her seven daughters."

"Wait a second," Scott added. "Wasn't Evita the wife of your president?"

"Oh, you silly *cucaracha,* you must not believe everything you see in the movies."

Scott scratched his head and shrugged.

Jessica let out a deep breath. *This is like being back in history class,* she thought. *Only I'm the one with the answer sheet! Luckily Liz is still off in another world, or else I'd probably be demoted to kindergarten.*

Lila cleared her throat and put on her most courtly smile. "Perdita . . . um, may I call you that?"

Jessica stuck her chin into the air. "But of course. We are among friends, is that not true in this case?"

Lila beamed. "We would be honored if you would consent to play in the mixed doubles tennis tournament we're having here at the club."

"Tennis?" Jessica repeated. She raised one thinly tweezed brow. "Is that an underwater sport?"

"No," Lila quickly responded, her eyes widening. "In this country we play on special courts on dry land."

"Ah, *sí,* courts, such as we use back home to be presented to the queen."

"Uh, no." Lila bit her lip. Jessica had to suppress a giggle as she watched Lila frantically looking around the table for help.

"It's when you hit a ball back and forth over a net," Anderson explained.

"Ahhh!" Jessica exclaimed. "I see. In the more civilized countries we call that *racquette.*"

"Exactly!" Pepper spluttered. "I *knew* that. Mumsy always called it *racquette.* Lila, we *must* change all the sign-up sheets. We're playing *racquette* from now on, not that horrible plebeian game called *tennis.*"

Jessica grinned. They were eating out of the palm of her hand! "That sounds lovely. Does it not, Cheep?" She turned to Nick, who was sitting beside her, practically dumbfounded. His mouth tightened and he gave an almost imperceptible shake of his head.

She frowned. Why wasn't he jumping at the chance? Playing in the tennis tournament would be the perfect in.

"Darling," he finally croaked. "Remember your jewelry."

Jewelry? Jessica thought. *I can take it off.* She made a face and started to open her mouth. But Nick pulled her toward him.

"I can't play tennis," he hissed into her ear. "Get us out of it. Tell them it's because of your bracelets!"

Jessica sat back, putting on a fake laugh. "Of course, I can be so . . . how do you say . . . *frivolous* sometimes. Cheep has reminded me that these lovely bracelets would get in the way." She held out her arms displaying the thick gold cuffs around her wrists. "Another time perhaps?"

Lila nodded, looking disappointed, but too thrilled to be in the company of Perdita del Mar to push it. "Oh look," she cried. "There's my boyfriend, Bruce, and our friends Bunny and Paul. You must stay and meet them, please."

"Of course," Jessica enthused. "We'd love so much to meet *all* your friends." *The more the merrier,* she thought. *Now all we have to do is figure out which one is the murderer!*

I can't believe Jessica's pulling this off, Nick thought, nervous sweat trickling down his back. He pulled on his collar, loosening the top button of his white oxford shirt. *With the stuff she's making up about Argentina, I can't believe no one's seen through her act.*

But to his amazement, everyone at the table, with the possible exception of Elizabeth, was continuing to fawn over Jessica like she was royalty. Bruce joined them, taking a seat next to Lila. Nick could see that Bruce was obviously fuming about something. Moments later, another couple, whom Lila introduced as Paul and Bunny, came over and also took seats at the table.

Hmm, Nick thought. *Is it possible that whatever is bugging Bruce has something to do with Bunny and Paul?* Bruce wouldn't even look at the couple. And he scowled every few seconds as if a bad taste was recurring in his mouth.

Paul and Bunny started chattering away gaily, obviously quite taken with Perdita del Mar. Nick couldn't help notice the contrast between Paul's ridiculously large shorts and Bunny's slinky red halter dress. *Is this guy Paul for real?* he wondered.

"Oooh, I can't *believe* you're from Argentina,"

Bunny gushed. "Daddy simply loves Buenos Aires."

Jessica smiled. "Yes, as I was telling your friends, it is the city of *amore*."

"Oooh! Paul, we *must* go there for our honeymoon!"

"Anderson is flying me down to pick out my engagement ring," Pepper cut in. "Perdita says that's where all the really big diamonds are from."

"Paul," Bunny pouted, stretching out her hand to display a rock the size of a golf ball. "I need a bigger ring."

"Anything you say, old girl," Paul replied, leaning back in his chair and practically toppling over.

"And I want bracelets like Perdita's too," Bunny added with a huge toothy smile.

Nick cringed. These were the most vacuous, conceited people he'd ever met in his life. *But is one of them a murderer?* he wondered.

Jessica laughed throatily. "I'm afraid these gold cuffs have been in the del Mar family for centuries. My great-great-grandfather dug them out of the ruins of a nearby Mayan temple with his own two hands."

"Mayan?" Scott queried. "Aren't those the Indians that lived in Mexico?"

Jessica nodded vigorously. *Uh-oh!* Nick could tell another tall tale was being manufactured by her overactive imagination.

"These were made by a splinter tribe that

traveled along the Amazon," Jessica chattered on breezily. "Warriors. Very fierce people, yes? They put a curse on our family. That is why I must never take the gold bracelets off. *Ay,* we would all perish then—a most grisly death to end all most grisly deaths!"

"Wow!" Bunny, Pepper, Anderson, and Paul all cried in unison.

Oh, brother, Nick thought. *When snobs think there's an even* bigger *snob around, they'll believe anything they're told!*

He let out a small sigh, feeling himself begin to relax. Their plan was working perfectly. Jessica was keeping everyone enthralled with her over-the-top Eva Perón impersonation, leaving him free to study the club's members.

"Paul, I'm thirsty," Bunny whined. "Could you order us something to drink?"

"Of course," Paul said.

Nick watched as he attempted to snap his fingers, but instead ended up hitting Bruce in the face.

Bruce growled and pushed his chair away. "Keep away from me, Krandall!"

Lila reached out and patted Bruce's arm. "Paul didn't mean anything by it."

Nick couldn't help but notice the warning look she gave him. "Hmmm," he murmured, noting the apparent strain in their relationship.

Anderson snapped his fingers and a waiter appeared at their table.

Paul took over then. "Carlos, iced tea for everyone, *répondez s'il vous plaît.*"

Répondez s'il vous plaît? Nick repeated mentally. He wasn't exactly bilingual, but even he knew that stood for RSVP in French. Something that went at the bottom of a party invitation, not a drink order. He looked at Paul more closely. Was this guy that dense? But before he could follow the thought, Jessica had stepped back into the spotlight.

"Iced tea!" she gushed. "*Ay caramba!* We must take great caution. It was in iced tea that my great-great-grandmother—she found the poison potion that announced the first Mayan attempt on my great-great-grandfather's life."

"Oooh," Pepper and Bunny gasped in unison.

Jessica nodded gravely. "You are lucky in your country that you do not have such crime."

"Oh, but we do," Pepper blurted out. "I heard that the police are investigating the club right now!"

"No!" Jessica gasped, throwing a hand to her mouth. "Why would that be?"

Everyone looked around the table, shaking their heads. Was it Nick's imagination, or were all eyes now scrutinizing him and Jessica to see what their reaction was?

He did his best to appear as befuddled as the rest. But the sweat had started trickling down his back again. *Somebody at this table knows why the police are interested in the club,* he thought. *And I'd better find out who before he—or she—realizes that Jess and I are on their trail!*

Bruce growled under his breath as he looked at the astonished faces around the table. He knew *exactly* why the police were investigating the club. They'd obviously gotten reports about a tennis hustling scam!

He looked over at Paul and glared. Paul looked back at him and Bruce could tell he was laughing. *That's it,* Bruce thought. He vaulted from his seat.

"If you'll excuse me," he said, nodding around the table. "I have some business to see to."

Lila grabbed his arm. "Where are you going?" she asked, her brows knitted in concern.

Bruce smiled and mimed making a phone call before stalking away from the table.

He went straight to the phone at the far end of the patio and punched in the number of the local police. "'Allo," he said, disguising his voice with a British accent. "Please, you must 'elp me. I was robbed by Paul Krandall."

"Could you say that again?" the policeman on the line asked.

"Paul Krandall," Bruce repeated and then slowly spelled the last name. "'e robbed me at the Verona Springs Country Club."

"Sir, could you give us your name?"

Bruce began making crackling noises into the

phone. "Sorry, officer, I think we 'ave a bad connection. Paul Krandall robbed me and 'e's at the Verona Springs Country Club."

"Sir," the policeman replied. "We've got that, but how can we contact you?"

Again Bruce made the crackling noises, biting his lip to keep from laughing. "You better 'urry before 'e strikes again!"

He hung up the phone and bent over in a fit of laughter. *That'll teach you to hustle me, Krandall,* Bruce thought, straightening up and wiping a tear of mirth from his eye. *You can't mess with a Patman without suffering the consequences!*

Now I'm sunk for sure! Elizabeth thought. She could feel her face turning as red as a stoplight. *With the way I'm blushing, everyone is going to see I know something!*

But the harder she tried to look innocent, the hotter and brighter her face felt. *I've got to get out of here,* she thought. *At least long enough to compose myself.*

But then they'll really *suspect you,* a small voice inside her head countered.

Elizabeth stifled a groan and looked down at her hands. Unconsciously she'd shredded a paper doily in two. *Calm down,* she scolded herself. *They're going to get even more suspicious if you're fidgeting!*

Suddenly Lila turned to her. "Liz, do you know anything about this investigation?"

"Me?" Elizabeth managed to squeak, feeling the air squeeze out of her lungs. "Why would *I* know anything?"

"You're an investigative reporter," Lila explained. "Don't you have a shortwave radio in your Jeep or something? Isn't that how you reporters work? Always after a story?"

Elizabeth gave a small nervous laugh as all eyes at the table turned and focused on her—and felt her spine tingle as she saw Bunny, Paul, Pepper, and Anderson looking downright hostile. "Um, not anymore," she declared hastily. She looked frantically at Scott for backup.

Scott gave a more natural laugh. "Liz is on the *Gazette* now," he broke in smoothly. "Our paper is much more interested in the club's social scene than in police investigations." He leaned over and gave Pepper and Bunny a conspiratorial wink. "Unless, of course, the police are now investigating society gossip."

Thankfully, Scott's comment hit the mark. Pepper and Bunny fell into giggles and Paul and Anderson visibly relaxed.

"We could tell you gossip that would turn your hair white," Pepper tittered. "Do you see that woman over there? Nina Storey? She's had three husbands and each one mysteriously disappeared during the honeymoon. She has over three homes and nearly ten million dollars in the bank!"

"No!" Scott gasped, playing along. "Maybe

that's what the police are investigating!"

"And maybe Liz has pictures of the missing husbands in her shoulder bag right now!" Lila joked. "Come on, Liz, let's take a look."

"Yeah, Elizabeth," Anderson added, leaning across the table toward her. "Let's see what you've found out about the 'Honeymoon Heiress' and her 'Tragic Trio' of elderly grooms."

Oh, no! Elizabeth thought. She'd been so frightened about the group somehow connecting her with the police investigation that she'd almost forgotten about the stolen mail in her bag. "Don't be silly, Lila," she choked out. "All I have in here are my notes on the tennis tournament."

But suddenly both Pepper and Bunny had begun to giggle again. They'd stood and were now advancing upon her from around either side of the table.

Elizabeth practically fell off her seat. Now what was she going to do—run or fight them off?

To her amazement it was Perdita del Mar who came to her rescue. "Amigos," she said with a huge yawn. "This game of yours, it is tiring me."

Immediately, Pepper and Bunny were back in their seats, contrite looks on their faces. Lila was laughing nervously, staring over at Perdita like a puppy dog that hoped its scolding was over. And Anderson and Paul had begun a lively conversation about the stock market.

Elizabeth silently thanked the lovely Argentinean.

But I'd better get out of here if I want to avoid anymore confrontations, she realized.

"Excuse me," she mumbled, half rising to her feet. But as she did so, Perdita stood as well. Elizabeth practically bumped heads with the mysterious woman and in that instant their identical aquamarine eyes met through Perdita's sunglasses. Elizabeth felt her mouth drop open and it took every ounce of strength to keep herself from fainting.

Chapter Twelve

She is following me! Jessica realized with a start. *What should I do?* She'd hoped that when she and Elizabeth had excused themselves from the table, Elizabeth would make a beeline for the country club's front gates.

Go home, Elizabeth, Jessica silently pleaded with her twin. *I'm here on official police business. I can't stop to worry about those VIP's going after you!* Besides, her whole Perdita act was a lot harder to pull off when she had to be constantly checking to see if her twin suspected anything.

Jessica increased her pace through the entranceway of the clubhouse, not easy on six-inch heels. Elizabeth was close behind. *Leave it to Liz to be wearing flats,* she thought darkly.

She hesitated in front of an oversized oil painting of the country club's founder. Mr. Valentine Verona IV's imposing face stared down at her imperiously from above the ornate mantelpiece, his nostrils forever flared in disdain. *I guess looking like a total snob has always been a prerequisite to membership,* Jessica thought, stifling a laugh.

She toyed with the pocket of her flowered dress, hoping against hope that Elizabeth would sail past her. But Elizabeth also hesitated near the mantelpiece, studying a set of old framed blueprints.

Pretending to tire of the picture, Jessica began to mosey around the sitting area. Obviously, Elizabeth wasn't going to leave her alone. *But why?* she wondered. Was their cover blown? Or was Elizabeth just being a good investigative reporter who was simply curious about the sparklingly beautiful and witty Latina newcomer?

"One way to find out," Jessica murmured. She faked a right and then flew through the door leading into the formal dining room. Inside, she plastered herself against the wall, camouflaged by the heavy drapes. Elizabeth rushed in moments later, her head switching back and forth frantically. Jessica held her breath as her twin hurried toward the other end of the room where a door stood ajar.

"Whew," Jessica whispered as her sister disappeared. "No time to lose, though. Liz will be back the minute she realizes the trail's gone cold."

She dashed out the door she'd come in and bounded up the carpeted stairs two at a time. She ducked into a secluded ladies' room on the second floor to catch her breath. "It's a good thing Lila explained the layout of this place to me in loving detail," Jessica laughed. "Or I would *never* have known all these escape routes."

She was just lifting up her dark sunglasses to get a good look around the dimly lit lounge when Elizabeth came barreling through the door.

Drat, Jessica thought. *That's the trouble with trying to outsmart an identical twin. They think the same way you do.* She let the sunglasses fall back onto the bridge of her nose and took a tentative step toward the mirror. She couldn't very well let Elizabeth see her eyes. But in this diffuse light she'd have to be careful too. She didn't want to break her neck falling over one of the plush chairs that adorned the room, the outlines of which she could just barely make out from behind her smoky lenses.

She stumbled a little, but somehow reached the counter safely. She fiddled around in her faux alligator-skin bag until she found her lipstick.

"You'd better take off those sunglasses now, Jess," Elizabeth smirked. "Otherwise that lipstick is going to leave you looking like a circus clown."

Jessica ignored the crack. She would give her cover one last try. She turned toward her sister, one thinly-plucked eyebrow raised. "Jess?" she repeated, deepening her voice by two octaves and adding a Spanish twist. "Is that some sort of bizarre American *idiom?*"

Elizabeth put her hands to her hips. "Yes, *Perdita*, it means *sister.* As in 'you can drop the act now.'"

Jessica sighed and pushed up her sunglasses. "When did you catch on?"

Elizabeth let out a low whistle. "Not till we practically bumped heads. That's some getup. What have you done to your eyebrows?"

Jessica shrugged. "They'll grow back."

"And your hair?" Elizabeth countered.

Jessica gave a small giggle. "You know, I always wanted to try this. By the way, it *is* a myth that blondes have more fun. I've been having a ball."

"So I noticed," Elizabeth commented drily. "Just what *are* you up to?"

Jessica sniffed. Stopping Elizabeth in her tracks by telling her that she and Nick were working undercover was oh-so-inviting. But she'd promised Nick she'd keep it under wraps. "I should be asking you the same thing," she hurled back instead.

Now it was Elizabeth's turn to act coy. She stepped up to the mirror and took out her lipstick. "Like I told the table—I'm writing a piece for the *Gazette* on the mixed doubles tennis tournament."

Jessica laughed. "Yeah, right! As if my sister would ever waste her time on the society pages."

"It's true," Elizabeth insisted. She turned to Jessica, her blue-green eyes wide and innocent. "Scott and I are even signed up to play."

Jessica rolled her eyes in response. "I perfected

that innocent look, remember? By the way, you need to lower your lashes once or twice to make it *really* believable."

Elizabeth scowled. "All right. So maybe the tournament is a bit of a cover. But you still haven't explained what you're doing here. I assume *Cheep* is none other than Nick Fox."

"Listen," Jessica half-threatened, half-pleaded. "Both you and I will be in *big* trouble if the people downstairs get suspicious. So how about a deal? I won't tell on you if you won't tell on me."

Elizabeth grimaced.

Jessica smiled. "I take that as a yes."

Elizabeth nodded, sealing the pact between them. "And Jess," she added. "Thanks for coming to my rescue out there."

"Don't worry, *conchita,*" Jessica trilled, slipping back into her Perdita act. "As you say here in your country—you cover my back and I'll cover yours."

"How did you like the music?" Dana asked gaily.

Tom looked up from his folding chair in the garden gazebo and blinked. He'd been so lost in his memories that he'd barely realized the string quartet had finished playing. "Um . . . ," he murmured, his mind still lingering on the first time he'd seen Elizabeth running across the SVU campus, her golden blond hair shimmering in the sun. "It was breathtaking."

Dana's full, red lips turned up into a pleased smile as she slipped into the empty seat next to him. "I had a little trouble at the start of the Handel concerto grosso. But overall I think it went very well."

Tom stared at the stunning, talented woman sitting next to him, trying to clear his mind of the cobwebs of the past. *Dana's with me now,* he thought. *Not Liz. It's Dana I should be thinking about.* But no matter how much he tried to convince himself, his thoughts seemed to snap back to Elizabeth every chance they got.

Tom reached out and squeezed Dana's hand. "It all sounded like magic to me."

Dana's hazel eyes danced. She leaned toward him and pressed her lips against his. "You say the sweetest things," she sighed. She sat back and ran a hand through her thick, mahogany curls. "I've got to pick up some sheet music for tomorrow's performance, but then maybe we can go for a drive along the coast. My car or yours?" she said brightly. "Or how about if we go back to that lovely restaurant on the cliffs?"

Tom shook his head. "Sorry. But I'm going to have to go back to campus. I have work to do at the station."

Dana stuck out her bottom lip. "But I haven't had a chance to spend any time with you."

Tom laughed. "We were together all day."

Dana started toying with the buttons on his

shirt. "But I was busy performing." She bowed her head and looked up at him through her long, willowy lashes. "I want some you-and-me time. Just the two of us, being cozy."

Tom felt his back stiffen. This was the type of coy behavior that bothered him. Elizabeth would never play games like this to get his attention. *But then if Liz and I were still together, she'd have* all *my attention,* he thought.

"Dana," he said, pulling her to her feet as he stood up. "There'll be other days. I took the afternoon off, but now I really have work to do. With Elizabeth gone, I'm practically running the WSVU station single-handedly."

Dana snorted, her face the picture of petulance. "Figures. Somehow your ex-girlfriend always manages to wreck our good time." She yanked a loose thread from the hem of her short, checkered sundress.

Tom flinched and narrowed his eyes angrily. "Let's leave her out of this, OK?" He turned and started stalking toward the parking lot.

"Tom," she called, running after him. "Wait." She grabbed hold of his arm and pulled him around to face her. "I'm sorry." Tears glittered on her lashes. "But sometimes I feel that there are three of us in this relationship. Me, you, and Elizabeth. I wish there were only two."

Tom felt some of the tension slip from his shoulders as he stared into her eyes. Dana wasn't playing now. She really cared about him. "So do I," he murmured. He bent down and kissed her gently on the lips before turning away.

He could never tell Dana which two he meant.

"It's about time," Elizabeth muttered. She reached across the seat of the cherry-red Jeep she shared with her twin and opened the passenger door for Scott. "I was afraid you didn't get my message."

"I got it all right," Scott replied, making a face. "That waiter Carlos made a big point of presenting me with your note. First he announced to the whole table that I was wanted *privately.* Then it took me another ten minutes to convince Lila and her friends that the note had nothing to do with red-hot club gossip we'd 'managed' to dig up. But rather—" Scott gave her an impish grin— "that you were jealous of my attention to Pepper."

"Scott," Elizabeth wailed in protest. She was getting really tired of his boyfriend act. She leaned back, crushing her ponytail against the leather headrest. "I really wish you wouldn't—," she started to complain. But at the last minute she bit her tongue. Her complaints could wait. She had something much more important to talk to him about.

Scott smiled at her, running his hand through his blond hair. "This is very romantic," he commented, turning and looking out the window.

"Luring me out to this secluded part of the parking lot with a mystery note. Maybe I *wasn't* paying enough attention to you," he teased.

Elizabeth rolled her blue-green eyes. "Scott, please. We're on the job. If you can't take it seriously maybe we should . . . "

"OK, OK," Scott laughed. "I get the point. So what's so important I had to abandon my tea?"

"I've got something to show you," Elizabeth told him reaching for her shoulder bag.

As soon as her hands touched the manila envelope in her bag she started to shake all over again. "I . . . took this from the manager's office after my interview," she hesitated, still barely able to believe her crazy actions. *But with Tom and Jessica running around like loose cannons,* she reasoned, *Scott and I have* got *to get this mystery solved before somebody else gets hurt.*

Scott took the envelope and dumped the contents onto the dashboard. "This is mail." He picked up several old utility bills, two circulars for a pizza place, and a postcard. "These are all addressed to Manuel Coimbra. Who's he?"

Elizabeth shifted excitedly in her seat behind the wheel. "I don't know for sure. But he was a busboy who worked here until a week or two ago. He left without giving notice. The manager's receptionist is keeping this mail for him."

Scott frowned. "So?"

Elizabeth grabbed his arm. "That's the same

time the caddy was murdered! Don't you think it's strange that this guy should disappear at the same time?"

Scott blinked excitedly and snatched the first letter. "We've got to open this mail. It might hold vital clues."

"No, we can't!" Elizabeth cried. "It's bad enough I took it, but to open it would be a federal offense."

Scott groaned and tossed the utility bill back on the dashboard. "You're right. As it is we're going to have to sneak this envelope back into that office."

Elizabeth reached over and plucked the postcard from the dashboard. "We can still read this." She smiled and looked down at the official-looking card. "Wait a minute," she murmured. "They spelled his name wrong—with an 'o'."

"Man-oh-el?" Scott pronounced. "That must be a mistake. I've never seen it spelled that way."

"Me either. Look—this is a notice informing him that his voting location has been changed."

"So?" Scott asked. "That happens a lot. Districts get redrawn, or new municipal buildings are erected."

Elizabeth shook her head. "No. It doesn't make sense. I specifically overheard the receptionist tell the manager that Manuel Coimbra could barely read or speak English. I don't think he was an American citizen at all."

Scott narrowed his eyes. "You're right. He'd most likely be a resident alien."

Elizabeth turned to him, the tiny hairs at the back of her neck standing up, signaling her that they were on to something. "And resident aliens don't vote—do they?"

"Hey, old man," a cultured voice inquired. "Could you give me a hand?"

Tom turned to see one of the VIPs standing by a sleek looking black Porsche in the parking lot. "Sure," Tom offered. He recognized the young man as Paul Krandall—the comically bad tennis player from yesterday's tournament. "What seems to be the problem? I'm Tom Watts."

The young man blushed and moved his tennis bag to his left hand. "Sorry, forgot my manners." He reached out and shook Tom's hand. "Paul Krandall. I'm afraid I've locked myself out again."

Tom peered into the tinted window and sure enough, keys were dangling in the ignition.

"I must do this once a week," Paul sighed. "Can't seem to keep it straight that the keys go *with* you."

"Hmm," Tom murmured, scratching his head. The window was open about an inch. "I think I've got an old hanger in my car. We can bend it into a hook and then pull on the door lock that way."

"Good show," Paul blubbered. "I should keep one of those in the car."

Tom made a face. "But then it would still be locked inside."

"Oh, right," Paul agreed. "I'd need another one to get it out to use it."

"But . . . ," Tom began. "Never mind." He trotted off to his car, smiling to himself. This guy was definitely *in* at the club; plus Paul was such a dimwit, he'd probably let nuclear secrets slip. "The perfect source of information," Tom mused.

He returned with the hanger as a police cruiser pulled up and a uniformed policeman stepped out.

"Are you Paul Krandall?" the beefy policeman asked.

Paul gulped and nodded. "This is my car, officer. I'm breaking into it because I got locked out."

The policeman growled. "It's not about the car, sir. We've had a report that you robbed someone."

Tom watched as Paul's mouth dropped open. "Me? Who would I rob?"

"Would you show me what's in your bag, please?" the policeman asked.

Paul placed his tennis bag onto the hood of his Porsche and started pulling out the contents. One tennis racket, two cans of balls, an empty bottle of water, and a *huge* wad of money.

Tom's eyes widened and he let out a low whistle. He'd *never* seen that much cash in one place. Had Paul *actually* robbed someone?

"Can you explain this?" the policeman demanded, scooping up the money.

"Naturally," Paul told him. "I didn't steal that money—I won it in a bet. Ask Bruce Patman."

"Attention Bruce Patman," an officious-sounding female voice announced through the country club's paging system. "Bruce Patman, will you please report to the parking lot."

Bruce's eyes lit up. *This is it,* he thought. *This is when I get my revenge on Paul!*

"Not so fast," Lila said, gripping his arm before he could get out of his seat at the patio table. "What's that all about?"

The two remaining members of their lunchtime group, Pepper and Anderson, both raised their eyebrows.

Bruce widened his eyes innocently. "I don't know, but I'd better go see." He stood and with his back turned to Pepper and Anderson, rubbing his hands together gleefully. *This is going to be fun,* he thought.

"Bruce," Lila hissed in a low whisper. "You'd better not be up to anything that could threaten our chances at the club."

"Moi?" Bruce teased. "What could I *possibly* be up to?"

Lila narrowed her eyes. "You've been warned."

Bruce smiled and jauntily made his way toward the parking lot, images of Paul being led off in handcuffs dancing in his eyes.

At the edge of the gravel parking lot he spied the flashing lights of a police cruiser. "All right," Bruce cheered. "Justice will prevail!"

Bruce trotted up to the hefty policeman. "I'm Bruce Patman," he announced. "Hey, Tom, are you going to write up this story?"

Tom shrugged indifferently, but his eyes were on fire with curiosity.

The policeman flipped open his notebook. "Mr. Patman, could I have your attention please?"

"Sure," Bruce smirked, mugging at Paul. "Ask me anything."

The policeman consulted his notes. "Did you lose a large sum of money to Mr. Krandall?"

"Lose?" Bruce snorted. "I guess it depends on your definition. *I* call it robbery. He stole—"

"Wait a minute," the policeman cut in. "Are *you* the person who called the police station to report a robbery? The guy with the fake British accent?"

Uh-oh! Bruce hadn't been planning to reveal himself as the source of the anonymous call. But he couldn't very well lie to a police officer, could he? "That's right, I called. He stole my money."

"Was this before or after your tennis game?" the policeman asked, checking his notes.

"It was *during* our tennis game."

The policeman scratched his chin. "While your back was turned? You're saying Mr. Krandall took something out of your bag?"

Bruce started to feel a little prickly heat under his collar. "Not exactly," he hesitated.

The policeman took off his mirrored sunglasses and tucked them into his top pocket. He studied Bruce with a skeptical squint.

"So what are you saying, Mr. Patman? Did he hold you up with his racket? Did he raise it over his head to strike you? Or point it at you like a tommy gun?"

"Nothing like that," Bruce moaned in defeat. He could feel the sweat pouring down his back. This policeman was making him look like a complete fool!

"No, I didn't *think* so," the policeman spat, slamming shut his notebook. "I ought to run you downtown right now for filing a false police report. Do you know how many crimes—*real* crimes—I could be out there solving right now?"

"B-But—but—," Bruce spluttered. "He *hustled* me!"

The policeman rolled his flinty-looking eyes. "One college kid hustling another is *not* robbery, Mr. Patman. There was no crime here, except possibly *slander!*" He turned to Paul. "In fact, Mr. Krandall, if *I* were you, I would consider suing him for defamation of character. I for one would be delighted to stand up in court and give evidence on your behalf."

Slander! Defamation of character! Bruce blanched. *Lila's going to boil me in oil!*

"That's all right, officer," Paul said smoothly, winking at Bruce. "Mr. Patman has a reputation around the club as being a bit of a clown. I'm sure he'll behave himself after this."

"A clown!" Bruce exploded. "If I'm a clown, it's all *your* fault—*and* Lila's . . . " The words choked in his throat as Lila stepped out from behind the police cruiser. Her brown eyes were almost black with fury.

"Come on, *Bozo!*" she ordered, digging her long nails into his skin. "We have some behavioral problems to discuss!"

Gulp! "Are you sure you don't want to run me downtown, officer?" Bruce asked feebly. Compared with the verbal thrashing he was going to take from Lila, jail was looking better by the second.

Chapter Thirteen

Boy, oh boy, Tom thought, watching Lila drag Bruce up toward the clubhouse. *Bruce is going to wish he'd never made that call.*

"Sorry about that, Mr. Krandall," the police officer apologized.

Tom watched as he handed the wad of money back to Paul.

"Not a problem, officer," Paul replied. "It's nice to know our boys in blue are out there when we need them." He peeled off a twenty-dollar bill from the top of the stack and handed it to the policeman.

The policeman put his hands up. "I couldn't take that, sir."

Paul smiled and folded up the bill. "Think of it as a donation for the Police Benevolent Association." He tucked it into the policeman's shirt pocket.

"Well, in *that* case . . . " The officer grinned,

patting his pocket. "It would be unfair to the rest of the force to say no." He got back into his police cruiser. "See you later, boys," he called as the car rolled away. "Stay out of trouble."

Paul laughed, waving good-bye to the officer. "That ought to buy me some goodwill."

Tom grimaced. It had all appeared aboveboard, but somehow that exchange of money hadn't felt right. He turned to look at the wad of bills Paul was putting back into his tennis bag. With the twenty gone, there was now a ten-dollar bill at the top of the stack.

Tom felt the air fly from his lungs. *Am I crazy,* he thought, *or did I see the word* suerte *in my own handwriting in the corner of that top bill?*

Tom forced himself to breath and nonchalantly leaned against the hood of Paul's car, taking a furtive peek into the tennis bag. Sure enough, *buena suerte* was written across the ten-dollar bill on top of the stack of cash.

Paul noticed Tom staring and frowned. "What is it, chum? Got a bit of the gambler in you too?"

Tom swallowed hard. "Not me. Too rich for my blood," he babbled, stepping away from the Porsche. "But boy, talk about that Patman! People who don't have enough class or money to lose gracefully shouldn't gamble. There should be a law or something."

Paul smiled and zipped up his bag. "Hey, don't go away just yet. We still need to get my door open."

Tom wiped his sweaty palms on his pants. "Sure . . . it shouldn't take more than a few minutes." He bent down to where he'd left the piece of wire.

"More than a few seconds, you mean," Paul said, taking the hanger from Tom.

"Actually, it's a little tricky," Tom started to explain. "Maybe you'd better let me—"

But before he could move, Paul had stepped deftly toward the Porsche, expertly twisting the wire and swinging it in a single motion through the slightly open window. The end of the hanger found the door lock instantly. "Hey, what do you know?" Paul exclaimed, his voice strangely flat. "Beginner's luck, I guess."

Tom could only gape, open-mouthed, as Paul slid smartly behind the wheel and handed him the hanger. "Thanks. Couldn't have done it without you." He gunned the engine, spitting a trail of gravel behind him as he peeled out of the parking lot.

Tom stared after the car, not quite able to shake the feeling of uneasiness that had come over him. "What's *that* guy's story?" he mumbled, looking down at the twisted coat hanger in his hand. "For such a dimwit, he's got some pretty sharp moves."

But more importantly, he added, *how did the ten-dollar bill I gave to Carlos end up in his bag?*

* * *

"Scott, did you see what I saw?" Elizabeth asked excitedly. She felt a little like a spy, hiding out in her Jeep as the human drama of Bruce, Paul, Tom, and the policeman unfolded in the parking lot.

"Hmm?" Scott murmured. He was holding up one of Manuel Coimbra's envelopes to the afternoon sunlight streaming in from the front window of the Jeep. "I can make out Dear Occupant, enclosed is an exciting new offer." He tossed the letter onto the dashboard with the other contents of the manila envelope. "It's more junk mail."

"I mean about Tom and Paul," she said irritably.

"What about them?" Scott asked. "There was a misunderstanding with the police about a large chunk of money. Bruce got dragged off by Lila, and the police left."

Elizabeth shook her head, gnawing on her bottom lip. She'd seen and heard all that too. But there was something else. She knew Tom. Not as well as she once had, when they could practically read each other's minds. But there was still a charged connection between them and Elizabeth was sure she'd witnessed a change—though subtle—in his posture toward Paul. Tom knew something. And she was going to try and find out what.

She turned to Scott. "I'm going to talk to Tom."

Scott stopped her by taking hold of her arm. "Are you sure that's wise? From where I'm sitting, it looks like *we* know a lot more than *he* does."

Elizabeth nodded, pulling her arm free. She reached for the door handle. "I think he knows something too."

Scott leaned back against the leather seat and crossed his arms. "What makes you think he'll tell *you?*"

Elizabeth cringed and pushed open the door. She would take her chances. "Maybe I'll have to make the first peace offering and trade him our information," she replied coolly.

Scott rolled his eyes. "There goes our advantage."

"It's still *my* story," Elizabeth replied, slamming the Jeep door behind her.

Elizabeth walked between two Jaguars and came out onto the main part of the gravel driveway on Tom's left. She could see his handsome profile was lost in thought—his dark, sparkling eyes staring toward the exit where Paul's Porsche had disappeared.

"Tom," she called softly, trying not to startle him.

He turned and looked at her, his face immediately softening, a smile replacing his contemplative frown. "Liz."

Elizabeth smiled back. It was the first time they'd been alone since she'd come out of her faint in his arms outside of the greenhouse. For a moment, lost in his warm gaze, she forgot why she'd approached him or that there'd ever been any trouble between them. He seemed to be in the same state of suspension, because he reached out his arms as if to gather her up.

Suddenly a loud, gunshot like sound rang out—car backfire from the back of the parking lot. They both jumped, and the moment was broken. Tom shoved his hands in the pockets of his chinos. "Are you leaving?" he asked. "Or did you just arrive?"

Elizabeth frowned.

Tom laughed a little nervously. "I mean, we're in a parking lot. I assumed it was one or the other."

"Oh . . . yeah." Elizabeth giggled. "Actually I had to look at something in my Jeep and I couldn't help noticing you were talking to Paul."

Tom ran a hand through his thick, dark hair. "Having car trouble?" He kicked at a large stone with his sneaker. The movement brought him a step closer.

Elizabeth smiled. "Not exactly," she hedged. "More like I needed some privacy to check something out."

"Oh?" Tom asked, giving her a sideways glance. "What might that be?"

"Well," Elizabeth teased, enjoying their mental sparring. "It's something that *might* relate to this story. It would be a lot clearer if I knew what you and Paul were talking about." She swished her olive green dress around her legs, bringing her a step closer to him.

Tom laughed. "Well, I'd have to know what it was you were looking at first." He twirled a little, further reducing the space between them.

Elizabeth grinned, leaning in until she was right beside him. "I think I might be a better judge of that, since I have the goods."

Tom bent his head. Now they were almost touching. Elizabeth caught her breath.

"I'll tell you what I know," she murmured, "if you tell me what you know."

Their eyes locked. Elizabeth could practically hear their hearts beating excitedly in time. And it wasn't just over this story either. After all the confusion and misunderstanding between them, they were on the brink of joining forces again. *Kiss me, Tom,* she thought, her head spinning. *Kiss me now!*

"Those two are on to something," Jessica remarked under her breath. "I can feel it in my bones." She leaned further over the low patio wall to get a better look at Elizabeth and Tom below her in the parking lot. Their heads were bent close together. Jessica could tell they were cooking something up.

"Oh, Perdita," Pepper's grating voice called out. "Come back and join us at the table."

Jessica scowled. Socializing with the VIPs was not only turning into a dead end investigation, but all their snobby behavior was also getting her down in a *big* way. On top of that, she could tell Nick was beginning to have second thoughts. If they didn't come up with a lead fast, he might decide to drop their plan and go undercover as a busboy or something—leaving Jessica out in the cold.

"If only I could hear what Elizabeth and Tom were saying," she muttered. "Then I'd have something to tell Nick, and he would be proud he made me his partner."

"Yoo-hoo, Perdita! Anderson has a question about the diamond mines."

Jessica turned to glare in the general direction of the table where Pepper and Anderson had cornered her and Nick moments earlier. She'd had to take a breather. Perdita had become such a hit, she was literally being hounded. "I'll be right there," she started to snap, before catching herself and dropping back into her Latina accent. "Perdita will be with you in *uno momento*."

She turned back to study Elizabeth and Tom. "Too bad I can't read lips," she murmured. But she was pretty good at reading body language, and those two were definitely excited about something. *Maybe they're making up,* Jessica thought. *Their movements look almost like a mating dance I saw on one of those TV nature shows.*

"Perdita, *what* are you *looking* at?"

"Aaugh!" Jessica screamed, practically tumbling over the small patio wall. She grabbed hold of a protruding flagpole at the last minute to steady herself. She turned furious eyes on her harasser. "Pepper, you must not sneak up on people in that manner! Is that how you do things in your country? *Ay!*"

"Sorry!" Pepper cried. "It's just . . . you . . . weren't coming back to the table." The corners of her mouth drooped in disappointment.

Jessica took a deep breath, mentally willing herself back into the Perdita role. "*Conchita,*" she stressed, "in *my* country one needs private time to commune with the nature."

Pepper gulped. Then her eyes traveled to where Jessica had been staring. "But that's the parking lot. And isn't that . . . "

Jessica grabbed Pepper's arm, pulling her away from the scene. "We Argentineans find beauty in many spots," she chattered. "The line of a well-made car, the crunch of gravel underfoot, the lush smell of gasoline."

Pepper grinned, nodding her head in total agreement. "Me too! I'm always telling Anderson, 'let's not rush right in, let's linger in the parking lot for a while.'"

Honestly! Jessica thought. If Perdita told her that she loved mosquito-infested forests, Pepper would probably be on the first plane to Malariaville.

Jessica took her seat at the table and stretched a languid hand around Nick's back. "Chip," she sighed, "Perdita is getting tired. Perhaps you can take us back to *casa mía*."

Nick practically leapt from his seat.

"Don't go home," Pepper begged. "I'm sure Bunny and Paul are coming back. We can all have dinner together."

"Really, you must stay," Anderson insisted. "We'll demand the chef cook you coconut stew."

Jessica stifled a groan and she could tell by the set of Nick's jaw that he was doing the same. Another meal with the VIPs wasn't going to get them anywhere—and the frustration was sure to make Nick decide to give up on the investigation.

But if I can find out what Liz and Tom know, Jessica thought determinedly, *that'll make all the difference.* She got to her feet. "I'm sorry *conchita, señor,* but Chip and I must be off like the wind."

She grabbed Nick's arm and started for the parking lot. With any luck, they could catch up to Elizabeth and get her to spill the beans. *Then not only will I help solve this case,* she thought, smiling to herself, *but I'll also have a proven track record. Nick will have to let me work with him on* all *his cases!*

She wants us to be partners! Tom thought. He could barely believe what Elizabeth was offering. His heart swelled, beating wildly against his chest. They would be together again!

Elizabeth was standing so close to him he could smell the fresh citrusy scent of her blond hair. He breathed her fragrance deeply into his lungs, memories exploding in his head.

"Liz," he said hoarsely, his vision clouding over. In his mind they were back in the WSVU building. Elizabeth was cuddled in his lap, her arms wrapped tenderly around his neck, their lips exploring each others' passionately. He was stroking her hair, hugging her tightly against him. *I'll never let you go again,* he thought. *You'll always be mine.*

"So, darling," a harsh voice cut through Tom's thoughts like a knife. "Did you get that information out of Watts?"

Tom's eyes snapped open and a small groan escaped from between his lips. He felt as if he'd been punched. The scene before him was a lot like the one he'd been imagining, except the arms wrapped around Elizabeth weren't his. Scott Sinclair was embracing her from behind, his chin resting possessively on her blond head, his lips curled in a mocking sneer.

Tom staggered backwards, feeling the color drain from his face. "You were trying to trick me."

"No, Tom," Elizabeth cried out. "That's not what I was doing. I . . . " She made a show of trying to get out of Scott's embrace, but Tom wasn't buying any of it.

"Don't bother," he cut her off curtly, his hands

balled into fists. "Too bad your *boyfriend* showed up before you could worm the information out of me. But as it is—no deal." He turned on his heel and started charging toward his car.

"Tom, wait!" Elizabeth called after him.

But he ignored her, fighting back the flood of emotion that was threatening to drown him. *She was just using me!* his mind railed. *She never cared!*

He hurled himself into his car, slumping over the steering wheel as angry, disappointed tears crowded his throat. "That's the last time I make that mistake," he choked out. "I'll never trust Elizabeth Wakefield again!"

***With Jessica, Elizabeth, and Tom all working against one another, danger is sure to follow. Whose cover will be blown first? Find out in Sweet Valley University* #35, UNDERCOVER ANGELS.**

SIGN UP FOR THE SWEET VALLEY HIGH® FAN CLUB!

Hey, girls! Get all the gossip on Sweet Valley High's® most popular teenagers when you join our fantastic Fan Club! As a member, you'll get all of this really cool stuff:

- Membership Card with your own personal Fan Club ID number
- A Sweet Valley High® Secret Treasure Box
- Sweet Valley High® Stationery
- Official Fan Club Pencil (for secret note writing!)
- Three Bookmarks
- A "Members Only" Door Hanger
- Two Skeins of J. & P. Coats® Embroidery Floss with flower barrette instruction leaflet
- Two editions of *The Oracle* newsletter
- Plus exclusive Sweet Valley High® product offers, special savings, contests, and much more!

Be the first to find out what Jessica & Elizabeth Wakefield are up to by joining the Sweet Valley High® Fan Club for the one-year membership fee of only $6.25 each for U.S. residents, $8.25 for Canadian residents (U.S. currency). Includes shipping & handling.

Send a check or money order (do not send cash) made payable to "Sweet Valley High® Fan Club" along with this form to:

SWEET VALLEY HIGH® FAN CLUB, BOX 3919-B, SCHAUMBURG, IL 60168-3919

NAME ____
(Please print clearly)

ADDRESS ____

CITY ____________________ STATE ________ ZIP ____________
(Required)

AGE __________ BIRTHDAY ________ / ________ / ________

Offer good while supplies last. Allow 6-8 weeks after check clearance for delivery. Addresses without ZIP codes cannot be honored. Offer good in USA & Canada only. Void where prohibited by law.

LCI-1383-123